A Shadow ~of~ Love

Amy S. Cutler

Black Rose Writing | Texas

ISBN: 978-1-68433-940-2
PUBLISHED BY BLACK ROSE WRITING
www.blackrosewriting.com

Printed in the United States of America
Suggested Retail Price (SRP) $18.95

A Shadow of Love is printed in Garamond Premier Pro

*As a planet-friendly publisher, Black Rose Writing does its best to
eliminate unnecessary waste to reduce paper usage and energy
costs, while never compromising the reading experience. As a result,
the final word count vs. page count may not meet common
expectations.

Acknowledgements

I find myself in a strange and wonderful time, where the dream of who I want to be is finally catching up with who I am. A few simple thank you's and I'm on my way to completion.

My dream started to become a reality when I first stepped onto campus at Goddard College in Vermont. The magic there has a way of seeping into your bones and working on your desires in your sleep. I give my thanks to the friends I made there and the advisors and faculty that have helped this book reach the end point.

They say it takes a village to raise a good human. I don't know about that, but while writing is a solitary job, it certainly takes a village to finish a book. I'd like to thank everyone who took valuable hours of their time to read this story, give me their comments and suggestions, and cheer me on.

When I started writing this book, my husband, Brian, did not know that he would be my impromptu editor, and he has taken on the task with an amazing effort. We talk about the characters as if they are living people, and I'm so glad to have found a playmate who will make believe with me.

I thank my entire family, who have been patient with me during this process, giving me space and time to complete this project while I should have been at work or doing family things. My sister, Rebecca, and my mom and dad, and the entire Mount Peter Ski Area family, have my infinite gratitude.

Thank you to my copyeditor, Anne-Marie Rutella for polishing this story so well, to Lynn Else for encouragement when I needed it the most, and Kei Kullberg for the amazing photography of the house and barn where this story takes place- those photos gave me endless inspiration. And to Black Rose Writing, for saying yes. Best. Email. Ever.

After I graduated from Goddard, my village got even bigger, as I was invited to the World's Best Writing Group that has kept me writing when I don't feel like it, and I am consistently inspired by their amazing talent. Thank you for setting the bar so high.

And to Zach. Thank you for showing me, every day, the importance of living your truth. I hope these characters reflect at least some of that resilience.

Thank you.

A Shadow of Love

Prologue

1917

"For this is a gracious thing, when, mindful of God, one endures grief while suffering unjustly."

–1 Peter 2:19

Lillian watched at the edge of the tree line as Christian hanged himself.

Sickened by his weakness, she regarded him bawling over what she presumed to be a poem or a letter to her, sitting on the dirty wood of the barn floor, silhouetted only by the Betty Lamp that burned by his feet.

Feeling nothing but anger for him, she stood by as he climbed a wooden ladder up to the rafter and stepped onto the beam. It was too dark for her to watch him tie the rope. She didn't see the circles around his eyes as he lowered his head and said a quiet prayer for his soul. Squinting in the darkness, Lillian only saw Christian tumble from the beam, caught inches before his feet hit the floor by the noose around his neck. She heard his neck snap, thinking for a second that it was the crunch of someone stepping on a fallen stick beside her. Slowly, Lillian crept from the cover of the woods. It was dark, and as she looked up at the moon, the clouds that blocked its light seemed to hear her and parted. By the light of the moon, Lillian stepped into the open barn and stood before Christian's hanging body.

Her eyes darkened as she looked at him, swaying ever so gently, body involuntarily twitching as the life drained from it. Crouching down, Lillian picked up the paper that Christian had been writing on.

"You bastard," Lillian whispered. She crumbled the note and tossed it into the darkness of the barn. "You kill yourself over me, a simple woman," she told his hanging corpse. "And now I will live with that burden. I will live with people looking at me either with pity or with hatred. I will live while you float off to meet your maker?" The moonlight seemed to follow her movements. Lillian moved closer to Christian's body, and the light from the moon shone on his hands, which were bleeding from the roughness of the rope.

Angry, Lillian cocked her head at the sight of the blood and closed her eyes, as if listening to directions from the wind. She nodded once, deciding.

Whirling around, she stomped out of the barn and searched for a stick. Finding what she needed, she trudged quickly back into the barn, her long skirt billowing around her ankles, dirty around the hem. She worked quickly, using her double-edged athame to slice at the wounds on Christian's hands, producing more blood. Blood immediately stuck to the blade. She dipped the point of her stick into the blood and drew a circle, the red blood mixing with the dirt on the floor. Inside that circle, she drew a pentacle and stepped into the circle of power.

Wind kicked up her long brown hair as she held her hands out to her sides, palms up, as if offering something to the heavens. Yelling above the wind, Lillian directed her words to Christian's body. "A lifetime of suffering times two, you, Christian Boyd, will be bound to this earth. For one hundred years your spirit will suffer on this land." Lillian closed her eyes and raised her face toward the sky, feeling the power swirl around her. She repeated, "A lifetime of suffering times two, you, Christian Boyd, will be bound to this earth. For one hundred years your spirit will suffer on this land." The moon shone brightly as coyotes howled all around the outside of the barn. Again, Lillian shouted, "A lifetime of suffering times two, you, Christian Boyd, will be bound to this earth. For one hundred years your spirit will suffer on this land."

A white ball of light rose from Christian's body, beaming out through the cracks in the barn's siding. For a few seconds, that light swirled around him. Lillian opened her eyes and smiled. The light rushed through him, entering through the top of his head and exiting through his feet. As the light left his feet, it seeped through the wooden floor of the barn and into the earth underneath. The lamp snuffed out as the light left the barn.

"It is done." Lillian sealed the spell with those final words. Working by only the glow of the moon, she stepped out of the circle. Lillian tucked her long hair behind her ears and brushed away the drawing. Leaving Christian's note crumbled on the floor, she looked once more at his body and walked quietly out of the barn.

Lillian was free to live out the rest of her life. For Christian, however, the spell would not be broken. It doomed him to spend the next one hundred years as a spirit trapped on Earth, unable to move on and unable to love.

Chapter One

2016

"I am done looking for love where it doesn't exist.
I am done coughing up dust in attempts to drink from dry wells."
–Maggie Young

Hers was the softest voice I had ever heard. It sounded like a wind chime in the distance, beautiful but barely there, a whisper, yet perfectly clear.

"Annabelle, you need to wake up," was all she said to me. So soft, but strong enough to pull me from my dream and back into the world.

My eyes opened to the fading light around me. "Mom?" I said and sat up, feeling the kitchen floor under me. "Mom?" There was no answer. Of course not, there could be no answer. My mother had died years ago, and now Christian was gone, too, and at that moment I was completely alone for the first time since I walked through these doors.

This house has a certain hold on me. I don't know if it's the house, or the energy, or the spirits, but from the moment I saw the listing, I knew I wanted to live here. The listing had read "Naples, NY - Beautiful, renovated 1860 farmhouse with all the modern conveniences. Sits on 150 acres complete with apple orchard. Relax in the airy kitchen and watch the deer play on your lawn.

Throughout this 1,800 square foot, four-bedroom home you'll find original millwork and lots of mystery."

I knew I didn't really need such a large home, or so much land, but when I clicked on the listing and saw the photos, I felt like this was my home and it was waiting for me. With a fresh coat of white paint, the house seemed dressed up on the outside, yet kind of worn on the inside. Perhaps I was just desperate for a place where I belonged, for a home of my own that had no ties to the life I was running from, but I felt a deep connection. Maybe I thought I would feel safe, because who would ever look for me in the middle of nowhere, in an old farmhouse that looks like a family lives there and not a recently single woman, all alone? Maybe it was just because it's an enormous change from living in a city, and I thought that an unfamiliar environment would help boost my creativity, which had seemed stagnant for so long. Whatever the draw was, I certainly never expected the journey that I have had since walking through these doors.

When I awoke on the kitchen floor after hearing the sweet voice of my mother in the distance, I was not sure if I really wanted to be alive. My heart felt broken, a piece of it taken away, and I felt that to get it back, I had to leave my life behind. Only a few weeks have passed, and it seems like the fog is clearing and my memories are getting fuzzy. I want to grasp hold of them, but it's like trying to catch air; the moments just slip away. Certain things I will never forget. Christian's lips, when they finally met mine, the way his hand felt pressed into my lower back while we danced in the kitchen. The curve of his spine, as we laid in bed together, wondering at the miracle of us being able to be together at all, fingers touching, maybe not completely solid but close enough. His eyes, as clear and blue as a frozen lake, that seem to hold so much life, even though they were void of life completely.

I must sound like a crazy person. I probably am. I fell in love with a ghost, a ghost who tried to chase me away but ended up holding me in his arms. A ghost by the name of Christian who is now not a ghost anymore, but something beyond my reach.

The more time that passes between then and now, between the unreal and the real, the more I wonder where I go from here. The snowy season is ending, and as spring approaches, I feel like I'm reliving everything that has happened. I must go back to the beginning to sort this all out, to make sense out of this great love I have for a man who thought that love was the worst-case scenario. A man who wanted me out as I was coming in.

Chapter Two

"Nothing in the universe can stop you from letting go and starting over."
–Guy Finley

The day I first turned the doorknob to my new home, giving the door a little shove to get it open, felt like a rebirth for me. I was finally home. There was no more running, no more fighting, just the quiet greeting of a house that was all mine.

There is nothing like the welcoming feel of an old farmhouse to make you feel at home. Large but cozy, right away I felt like the house had secrets, but that seemed right to me. I had secrets of my own, and it felt comforting to be in a place that had a history.

The kitchen is the main hub of the house and where guests enter. There is a large table in the center of the room, and a fireplace, complete with two rocking chairs. It is the kitchen that is the heart of the home. The house had been on the market for years. I figured that it probably had some issues because of its age, but from the first moment I stepped into the kitchen with my Realtor—who seemed a little hesitant, looking back—I felt drawn to its old-fashioned charm. Once the house went through an inspection and no major problems came up, I never gave another thought to why it had sat on the market for so long at a comparatively low price. This was my home, and that was all that mattered.

The house came partially furnished, which was perfect because when I left my marriage, I also left behind all my furniture. While My parents and grandparents gave some of my belongings to me, I couldn't imagine ever sleeping in the same bed I had shared with Scott, or curling up in the easy chair that I had shed so many tears on. Better to have someone else's memories than relive my own.

On that first day, as I walked through my beautiful old home, I thought of Scott and wondered what he would think of me buying this place. He had the opinion that I was a weak and stupid girl and would never survive without him. Of course, I could survive without him; in fact, I believe it is the only way I can survive at all. My mind always goes to the darkest detail, and I told myself to stop it. I whispered, "Let it go" into the house, but in the empty room it seemed too loud. Self-doubt results from being emotionally and physically mistreated—something I learned in the many self-help books I have read. Although I know better in my heart, sometimes my head thinks that maybe he was right. I have read more self-help books than I wish to remember, but terms like *gaslighting* always come to mind when I think back on our marriage, and reading that abusive behavior like that is a real thing—with a real term—made me feel better as I was reading about it. Scott always made me feel like I was crazy, or wrong; if we had an argument about something, I would always end up apologizing. He could take any topic and twist words around and talk in circles until I just assumed that I was an idiot, and I made a mistake. He would blame me for everything, from his jeans being too tight after I washed them, to him leaving his keys on the kitchen table and locking himself out of the house—when I wasn't even home.

I will always remember that first afternoon, exploring inch by inch. I was completely in love and felt free. After circling the entire kitchen and soaking in everything that I saw—the wooden fireplace mantel waiting for photos and a painting on top of it, washer and dryer, broom closet, cabinets—I went around touching everything I could. There is a couch along one wall that I sat on for about three seconds before venturing over to a cabinet with an ancient radio that did not turn on when I tried it. Through the other end of the kitchen is a door that opens to steps to a bedroom on the second floor. I took them two at a time, and memorized all the tiny details: the empty twin beds, each by a small window, which were under the sloped ceiling, so that if you sat up too quickly, you would bang your head. The small bathroom is quaint, with a broken fan that noisily squeals when you pull the chain.

If I thought the inside of the house was special, the outside was stunning. With everything in full bloom from the apple trees to the giant Oaks that outlined the property, I felt like I had didn't deserve such beautiful property for what I paid for it. I wondered for the first time if fate, or the universe, or some larger force had brought me here as part of my life's journey.

As I wandered through the house, I couldn't help but remember when Scott and I first looked at our condo together. He was so romantic and considerate, even making the small loft area into a tiny library for me to write in. Our condo was in Rochester, which was perfect for me, a community news reporter who traveled to events in the area when I was working on a story. I loved being in the center of the stories I was writing and the community that I was covering.

After a while, though, the more controlling Scott became, the more air I felt like I needed. It was as though I was suffocating in a big city, in a tiny condo. Especially after I started my own column featuring the city's shelter pets. Scott became more possessive, and it felt unbearable for me to stay there. This house felt like freedom to me, with all the empty rooms and windows that looked out at nothing but trees and open space.

I did not know what to do with four bedrooms, but I really didn't care. One would make a pleasant office, and I'd make one a guest room, since I was sure my sister, Nancy, would eventually visit. We used to be so close after our parents died—I actually used most of my inheritance to buy this house—but she grew impatient with me once I moved in with Scott; I would often cancel our plans to meet up, or forget to return her calls. One day, I may have the courage to tell her the truth. After my recent brush with death, I have a whole fresh interest in opening up and forming a better relationship.

After my tour of the upstairs, I went down the main steps to the ground floor and stepped into the small living room—what would have originally been known as the parlor. The room is small but cozy, with its own fireplace. Attached to that room is the primary bedroom, with a queen bed and cabinets built into the wall. The house doesn't have a lot of closet space, but that was okay, since I didn't exactly arrive with a lot of belongings. The best part of the house is a newly remodeled main bathroom with stone tile, all bright and new and shiny. I remember just standing in the bathroom on that first day, taking in deep breaths and ever so slowly letting them out. I felt safe and content.

As I got to work unpacking my SUV, I was suddenly so tired. Although I had little belongings, I still filled my car to the brim. On my first trip back into the house, I stopped to look up at the barn. About 100 yards from the house and just past a little cluster of apple trees, the large structure sort of loomed up on a hill. Not quite falling but not quite pristine, I could see right into the top, which I guessed which was a hay loft area. My eyes lingered for just a moment on the beam that ran from one end to the other, and I had to squint to focus on the tiny black objects that I saw darting about from the inside. It was just getting dark, and the bats were out.

Super-duper, I thought. *Bats live in the barn. Well, I guess I'll be staying out of there when the sun goes down.* I hate bats, the way they swoop down from nowhere, and I could just imagine myself going for a little moonlit stroll and getting attacked by the little winged creatures.

. . .

Sixteen bags, two hours, and about half a bottle of wine later, I collapsed on my bed. The mattress was old and creaky, but I had purchased new sheets from Walmart on my way, and it felt so good to lie down. I found myself wishing again that I hadn't let my friendships drop off when Scott started becoming jealous and controlling. I missed my friends, and I missed spending hours talking to my sister Nancy on the phone. And right about then, on that first night, I missed having the help and company of people who loved me.

Even though I felt exhausted and thought that I would pass out as soon as my head hit the pillow, I lay in bed, eyes open, thoughts racing. With no television in the house to occupy my mind, I got out of bed and sat on the floor, pulling over a half-opened box of photo albums and old journals. I couldn't stand to look at photos of Scott, but I flipped back to before we met and felt surprised by how much different I was. Younger, of course, since we had been together for fifteen years, but there was such innocence in my expression. There was a photo of me and Nancy, who is six years older and practically raised me after our parents died. I was young, only seventeen, but she was permitted to be my official guardian. Nancy's hazel eyes were brighter than my own, her hair a darker shade of brown, almost black. I couldn't help but stare at one photo that showed both of us standing next to each other, arms over each other's shoulders, smiling on the beach with waves behind us. Looking at that photo, I thought I would do anything to go back to that day, and go back to my hotel room for a nap instead of to the bar, where I met Scott for the first time. I pulled the photo from the plastic sleeve and hugged it to me.

Although it was late—almost midnight—I picked up my cell and considered calling Nancy. She knew I had left Scott, of course. She said I was crazy for buying an old house in the middle of nowhere, but she knew better than to try to talk me out of something once I set my mind on it. Nancy knew I hadn't been happy in my marriage, and we had talked about some issues, like emotional abuse, which she had apparently seen in my relationship before I did. But I never told her he hit me. It's not that I don't trust her or have an idea that I can do everything on my own, but it embarrassed me, like it made me a weak person to let someone do that to me. In hindsight, I see that reasoning is all part of being abused. I just couldn't say those words to her.

I also knew that she would be eager to hear from me, and I realized, not for the first time, how far I had drifted from my sister, because just a few years ago I would have asked for her help, and we would unpack my belongings together.

My fingers hovered over the numbers on the phone when I realized I had no service. I supposed I would have to get a landline at some point, as well as hard-wire my computer so that I could have internet and work. I climbed back into bed for another attempt at sleep.

It is hard work to sort through your past and focus on the future all at once, and suddenly I was exhausted. Moments after I laid back down, my eyes got heavy, and I had that drowsy feeling that one gets after an emotional day followed by physical exertion and too much wine. I thought I was asleep and dreaming, but now I know that as I was drifting off, I heard a whisper pass by my ear.

"What are you doing here?" the whisper asked.

Unfazed, almost asleep, I clearly remember answering, "I'm moving on," before falling into a deep, dream-filled sleep that I can remember only as fragments. The one image from that dream that has stayed with me was a man gasping his last breath as a piece of rope choked off his air supply. One boot lay on a dirty barn floor below his hanging body, his foot bare and twitching in the moonlight.

Chapter Three

"It's okay to be crazy and scared and brave at the same time!"
–Kelly Epperson

As a freelance journalist who can submit stories from anywhere, I hardly remember what it is like to go into an office every day. I usually work from home. I can work from wherever I want to, actually; the beach, a hotel room at Niagara Falls, once from my bathroom floor. I had been living in the house for about a week, and had started to set up one bedroom upstairs as an office—complete with working internet after having the cable guys in my house for hours—and was about to sit down to work on my newest column idea, Taking Care of Yourself in Times of Crisis, when Scott called me. I had to go downstairs to answer, given the poor reception on the second floor.

In hindsight, I never should have answered his calls. Before I could even say hello, he was talking. "Annabelle, baby, you have to let me come see you. I can't stand this," he pleaded. Immediately, I regretted answering, but I knew he had received the divorce papers and I wanted to move things along.

"Scott, please, I've given you everything I had to give. Please sign the papers so we can move on with our lives." I was on my cell, pacing the house, and cursing the signal. My cell was always cutting out, and I made a mental list to get the landline that I had declined to save money.

He laughed at me, changing his tone from pleading to threatening, as usual. I was dismissing him, and he couldn't stand that. "Give me your address, Annabelle. I have a right to see my wife."

Nothing frightened me more than Scott finding out where I lived. I knew he would do anything to get me to come back to him and wasn't always sure if it was the angry Scott or the crying Scott that frightened me the most. Hearing him call me his wife gave me the creeps. I told him he has no reason to know where I live, and my post office box number is all he needs. His tone became softer, which made me even more uncomfortable than when he was angry, as he told me, "I do need to see you, love. I miss you, I'm sure we can work this out."

I rolled my eyes, feeling brave and combative since I felt safe out of his distance. "Scott, I told you that it was over." And, rehearsing a line that I had read in one of the many books I had read on ending a marriage, I said, "I'm sorry if you don't understand, but..."

He cut me off, telling me fine, he didn't give a shit about our broken marriage anyway, he just wanted some of his belongings back.

"What belongings?" I asked him. When I left, I had taken only what was mine, nothing that we shared. I took my clothes and personal items, and the one gift that his mother had given to me before she passed, a beautiful sunflower painting that she had painted just for me. "You're not talking about the painting, are you? That was a gift for my birthday."

The line went dead. "Hello? Are you kidding me?" I said into the silent phone. I didn't know whether it was my phone or if he hung up on me. Of course, nothing more had been resolved, and I was no closer to Scott signing the papers than I was before the call.

As I chucked my phone onto the counter next to the kitchen sink, I saw my reflection in the big picture window that overlooked a picture-perfect field. There was a deer munching on an apple under an apple tree, which made me pause long enough to take a few shaky breaths.

Still gazing at both my reflection and the doe, noticing what a mess my hair was in the bun I shoved it in, I whispered, "Asshole." I didn't know if I meant Scott or myself. I turned on the faucet and filled my hands with cool water, splashing my face. Trying to center myself, I pictured the painting, propped up against a wall in an upstairs bedroom. I loved that painting because I had loved his mom before she passed, but I put it away in a spare room because I was not ready to look at anything from my life with Scott just yet.

With my eyes closed, I felt around the counter for the paper towels, but stopped short, hairs on my arms and the back of my neck standing on end. The room got about twenty degrees colder, and even though I knew I was alone and had locked all the doors, I felt like someone was watching me. Just as my fingers found the paper towels, and I tore off a strip, the ripping sound loud enough to give me chills, my cell rang, causing that ripple of fear traveling down my spine and into my feet.

My eyes shot open, and I grabbed the phone. I couldn't answer it, though, because it was not on. The screen was black, and when I tried the button on the side, the screen flashed *low battery* and turned off again.

"Okay, that was freaking weird," I said, looking around for the source of my unease. Nothing was out of order, and even though my skin felt cool, the room was warm again. I wondered if the stress of talking to Scott caused some reaction in my body. "I think I need to take a walk. And maybe get a dog." At least with a dog, I thought, I wouldn't really be talking to myself.

Searching for my sneakers, I crossed the kitchen to look by the front door. I told myself that I would put them on outside to get some fresh air, but really, I knew that I just did not want to be in the house at that moment. I grabbed my shoes and had my hand on the doorknob when I glanced at my phone, and saw that it had blinked on and the screen read *100% charged*.

I shook my head, and just as I was about to yank the sticky door open, a face appeared on the other side of the window. Someone was standing on my front stoop. I let out a scream. Realizing it was an actual person, I opened the door and laughed at myself. I greeted an older, gray-haired woman carrying a basket of fruit.

"I am so sorry," I told the woman. "I did not even hear a car pull in."

The woman smiled at me—her face wrinkling up so that her laugh lines spread to her ears. "Oh, honey, I'm so sorry to startle you. I walked here. I saw you had moved in and wanted to welcome you. My name is Elizabeth, but my friends call me Lizzy. And that is what you should call me."

We shook hands, and Lizzy handed me a huge fruit basket—filled to the brim with apples, bananas and orange, one orange twice the size of the others - and as I took it from her, I heard the soft jingling of her bracelets. I guessed Lizzy was in her seventies, although her outfit choice—a long, flowing patchwork skirt with an equally colorful peasant top—definitely made her look hip.

I was delighted. It had been a while since I'd seen a friendly face. "Thank you so much. My name is Annabelle Peterson, and you may be my very first friend here," I said, smiling at Lizzy.

"I live just two doors down, in the little modular." Lizzy pointed down the road toward her house. "So, if you need anything, don't hesitate to drop by. And how you are you, ah, getting along here?"

"Getting along?" I asked her, laughing nervously. "I guess okay. Although as you can probably tell, the quiet has me a bit jumpy."

I noticed that Lizzy kept glancing up at the house. "Well. I truly hope that this house lets you stay. You seem like such a nice person."

"What do you mean, you hope the house lets me stay?" I asked, glancing over Lizzy's shoulder as if someone might hear.

"Oh nothing, really." Lizzy dropped her voice to a whisper. "It's just that whenever someone moves into the house, they seem to hightail it right back out of town, mumbling about the place being haunted. I'm sure that's not the case. Maybe the heating bill was just higher than they were expecting," she told me, winking.

"Well, I don't believe in ghosts," I told her, straightening myself up a bit.

"I'm sure, dear, and neither do I, although my mother has told me some stories about the place that would make your skin crawl." I think she finally realized she was making *my* skin crawl, and backpedaled a bit. "Of course, I'm sure they are all just stories."

"Well, thank you so much for dropping by, Lizzy. It's been, ah, eye opening."

As we shook hands to say goodbye, Lizzy told me she owned the coffee shop in town, called Aunt Lizzy's. "Please, stop by anytime. Next Thursday we are having a poetry reading at seven o'clock. You should come."

"You know what? I think I will. I love poetry," I told her. Lizzy turned to walk back down the driveway, smiling at me as if we were old friends. It was weird, and welcoming, and I wasn't sure if Lizzy was kidding about the house being haunted or not.

I wasn't sure why I had lied to her. I think maybe I didn't want to be spooked in my new home, and I really didn't want to talk about it. The fact is, I do believe in ghosts, and in the afterlife, and that spirits can communicate in all sorts of ways. I actually practiced Wicca throughout my late teenage years and into my twenties, and while I had traded a life of incantations and circle gatherings for marriage and a life that Scott felt was "more ordinary," the truth of the matter was that I was slowly realizing that I may have been drawn to the house and felt at home here because it tied me to my old life, my life before Scott.

I suddenly felt pretty stupid for not seeing the signs that something was up. The fact that the house was vacant for so long and sold at below market value should have been a big indicator. I guess I had been ingrained in Scott's world for so long, where I focused on the here and now, and on the tangible, touchable parts of life while trying to ignore what I had been so fascinated with, that I ignored what was right in front of me.

I quickly went inside and put the basket of fruit on the counter. As I went back out to the front step and tied my shoes, I decided I could use a jog rather than just a walk. Did I feel that someone was watching me as I ran off down the street? I did not think it then, but looking back, I may have felt a twinge of something in my consciousness.

I have always loved to exercise. Whenever I feel super stressed out, I put on my sneakers and head outdoors, no matter the weather. The endorphins pumping through my body make me feel good, and that day in particular I was happy to have the distraction of a new view to enjoy. Even though New York gets hot in the summer months, there are also glorious breaks in the heat where it feels almost like an early fall, and the weather that day was perfect. I ran all the way to the chicken farm about a mile down the road, enjoying the bright red barns and country air. By the time I got back to the house, I had shaken off the funky feeling that I had. *This is my house now,* I told myself. *And my house will only have good energy.*

After a huge salad and a glass of wine for dinner, I took a hot shower, enjoying the dual showerheads. Todd, my realtor, had told me that the last owner wanted to update the entire house, but ended up moving out soon after he finished with the bathroom. I love my bathroom, but am glad that they didn't get a chance to update the rest of the house. It is charming, and as I got into bed that night, I just breathed in the scents of wood and old memories. This house had to have a lot of them. Only then, I didn't know how close I was to getting a pretty intimate history lesson.

chapter four

"Within its gates I heard the sound
Of winds in cypress caverns caught
Of huddling trees that moaned, and sought
To whisper what their roots had found."

"A Dream of Fear"

–George Sterling, *The Thirst of Satan: Poems of Fantasy and Terror*

The windows rattled and the sound of the rain made me think of long, bone-white fingers tapping on the glass. The clock beside my bed read 12:12 a.m., and although I was worn out completely from my run earlier that day, not to mention another ridiculous argument I had with my soon-to-be ex-husband, I could not coax my eyes shut.

The living room clock ticked softly, and as 12:12 slowly became 12:30, I finally settled into the rhythms of the storm, letting my eyes grow heavy as I counted the seconds between the thunder and the lightning, and I fell asleep.

As the night wore on and the storm raged outside, a man softly calling my name roused me. From the depths of my sleep, I heard it, as if someone were in the next room. "Annabelle... Annabelle..." came the voice.

Unthinking, I answered, "Yes?"

At the sound of my own voice, however, I shot up into a sitting position, heart beating abnormally fast. "It was a dream," I whispered. Looking up at the clock to see that it had stopped at 1:42, I wondered briefly if I was going crazy and imagining things, or if maybe this house really was haunted. I believed in ghosts, but didn't really want to think about them in the middle of the night. I had felt so strong when buying the house, but I never imagined that I could feel so independent and frightened at the same time.

Breathing in and out as slowly as I could, I told myself over and over, "It's just the storm. It's just the storm."

As I closed my eyes, I heard that damn tapping on the window again, the one that made me think of white fingers tapping on the glass. A tree branch, or a stick, is what I knew it was. But the sound was enough to keep me from closing my eyes for more than a few seconds. Thinking that a little cool water would help shake the horrible feeling of being watched, I got up and went into the bathroom. I shut the door behind me and turned on the light. Only it wasn't my newly refurbished bathroom I was stepping into. The beautiful tile floor was now thick wooden planks, the walls were peeling paint, and the toilet, sink, and shower were no longer there. The entire bathroom was just an empty old closet.

A shiver made its way up my spine.

Feeling fully awake now, I turned around in the small room and grabbed the door handle to get out of there, only to find myself standing in the living room of the house I lived in, only much, much different—like I had traveled back in time.

I didn't exactly know I was dreaming, but also did not feel terribly surprised by what I was seeing. The storm had stopped, and daylight streamed through the windows. The clocks were all stopped at 1:42. My living room had been transformed into the more traditional term of a parlor. A small organ piano sat in one corner. Candles and photos were propped in another. And at the far end of the room, the body of a woman was laid out in a handmade casket.

A man, presumably the husband, sat in a wooden chair next to the casket. A young girl—wearing the formal mourning attire of a black dress and veil—quietly spoke with the guests. What stood out the most for me, though, was the young boy sitting in the corner, tears dripping down his chin.

The man spoke to the boy gruffly. "Christian," he said, and the boy sat up straight. "Your mother would not approve of you sitting on the floor. Go on, get up, be respectful."

"Yes, Pa," the boy answered, wiping his nose on the back of his hand but not bothering to hide his tears. "Sorry."

The young Christian got up and politely moved through the house, past the guests, and as soon as he could, ran upstairs to his bedroom. Somehow, knowing they could not see me, I went to the body. In the casket lay a beautiful woman, with silky black hair and high cheekbones. The woman's lips were slightly parted, and her face looked relaxed.

Wanting to escape the sadness of the room, I went up the stairs and into the bedroom with the slanted ceiling, where I heard Christian softly sniffle. I wanted to console the boy, but was afraid to speak to him, so I sat next to him on his small bed. Of course, he could not see me, but nevertheless, I wanted to stay. I felt like it was the right thing to do.

I didn't know how much time had passed, but it had gotten very dark out. The storm started up again, this time with thunder shaking the single-pane windows. It was peaceful enough, sitting there with the drowsing boy, until the noise. We both heard it at the same time; a low, guttural groaning sound coming from the room below. Christian shot up like an arrow and before I knew what was happening, we were both standing in the living room.

The first thing I noticed was the smell. It smelled like a mixture of bad indigestion and rotting meat. And then the sound came again, through the lips of the body that were parted even further than earlier. A growl, louder this time, followed by a slight sinking noise as the corpse's chest collapsed. I felt my heart kick into high gear. My fingers went numb. I couldn't move, couldn't run away, but Christian could move just fine. I watched in horror as he slowly walked toward his mother's casket.

"Mama?" he cried. He slowly reached out to take her hand. His fingers brushed the lace of the dress they would bury her in. Her arm shot straight out and hovered there in the air, as if reaching out for her son.

Christian screamed the scream of an animal going in for slaughter. It wasn't a child's scream; it was a scream of terror. A scream that would bounce off these walls for the next one hundred years.

I instinctively squeezed my eyes shut and covered my ears, screaming right along with him. I screamed until I woke myself up, sweating in my bed, heart thundering to the beat of the storm. The clock read 1:43, and after a dozen or so panicky breaths, I finally realized that I had been dreaming.

I reached for my nightstand lamp and turned it on. Not bright enough for me, I got up and turned on the bathroom light and was happy to see that my bathroom was still perfectly intact; new tile and everything. I didn't go into the living room, though. Although I knew it was a dream, or rather a terrible nightmare, I knew I couldn't face that room again until the sun was up.

The worst part about that night was not the nightmare. That was scary, but what was worse was lying in bed, too afraid to go to sleep and too afraid to get up, straining to hear any sound in the house. What I heard, when I listened past the rain and the thunder, was a creaking of the floor in the kitchen. It sounded like the rocking chair in front of the cold fireplace, rocking back and forth. Back and forth.

Chapter Five

"With a library it is easier to hope for serendipity than to look for a precise answer."
–Lemony Snicket, *When Did You See Her Last?*

The next week seemed to drag on. Every time I closed my eyes, I wondered if I was going to have another strange nightmare. Walking through the parlor turned into something I didn't mind doing only during the daytime, which was difficult since I had to enter and exit each time I went into my bedroom. As the days went by, I couldn't shake the feeling I had. It was plain old heebie-jeebies. I could not quite relax. Each time I sat down to work on my column for the paper, I found myself turning to look behind me.

I ignored two emails from my editor, and when he left me a voice mail saying, in the clipped tone that I had only heard him use with other writers, "I know you are going through some stuff but it's been over a month. There is a statute of limitations for recovery time, Annabelle," I emailed him and promised that I would turn something in within the next few days.

I know that old houses creak and groan, but couldn't help wondering if it was just an old house settling its joints, the wind outside, or something else—perhaps a chair being pushed around, or footsteps in the hall.

More and more, I thought of the little boy from my dream.

I also wondered about the woman who was being mourned in her living room, or, to be accurate, the parlor. I couldn't imagine sleeping under the same roof as your loved one who had died. I knew that embalming is a relatively recent practice, and I thought about the indignity of leaking body fluids while your neighbors came calling.

Sleeping was becoming more difficult, as bad dreams were taking over my slumber. Just a few nights after the first bad dream, I had another one that sticks with me. This was not as vivid as the first, but I have clear images of being in the barn, and someone was calling my name from the rafters above my head. When I looked up, I saw a man falling, but instead of hitting the ground, there was a rope around his neck and he stopped falling just inches before hitting the dirty wooden floor, neck snapping at the last moment. In the dream, at one moment I was standing there watching this man fall, and in the next second, I was falling myself. I awoke with a start, covered in sweat and grasping at my neck.

I started to wonder if the dreams that I had been having since moving into the house were something more than an overactive imagination. It was starting to feel like I was actually seeing the memories of the house. The dreams seemed so real. The man hanging from the rafter in the barn, and the woman laid out in the parlor, were bad enough, but I also remembered having fragments of other dreams as well, dreams that just didn't make any sense to me. One night, before the nightmare, I dreamed I was a woman named Lillian, and I was having a fight with a man, right in my own kitchen. I can't remember much from that dream, but I remember telling him I needed to move on.

I also wondered about the house and its history. It was something that I hadn't thought about before, since when I bought the house, I was more concerned with the leaving of where I was than what the history of the house was, but now I wanted to know. I tried a Google search, typing my address, but nothing came up. I even tried, "Can you dream about someone else's memories?" but I shut my computer down in the middle of the search. The room grew cold, suddenly, and the internet seemed even slower than usual. Did the house not want me to have these answers? I wondered. That thought seemed silly. Even so, I felt uncomfortable about sitting in the quiet room, researching. Sighing at my computer, I knew I had to make a trip to the local library.

On the way to town, I called Nancy. Using the speakerphone on my cell, I maneuvered the back roads I was still learning while hoping I wouldn't lose service. Nancy answered on the second ring.

"Hey, sis," she said by way of greeting.

"Hey, Nancy. It's so nice to hear a friendly voice," I told her, already feeling guilty that it took me so long to call. It had been a few weeks since I moved, and although I checked in with her through a daily text, I couldn't bring myself to make an actual call. I still didn't want her to find out the real reason why I left Scott— as if him treating me like garbage wasn't bad enough. If she found out that he was hurting me physically, she would have confronted him, and I knew I couldn't keep that truth out of my voice if we spoke too soon.

"Well, I'd be even friendlier if you called more often. Or actually picked up your phone when I call you," Nancy said. She has always been like that, quick to be sarcastic. It is more of a defense tactic, as a way for her to hide her hurt. It made me feel bad, and I felt sorry that I wasn't better at talking to her.

"I know, I'm sorry," was all I could come up with.

"I still love you," Nancy told me. "And you should be proud of me for giving you your space. How's the house? You do realize you officially live in the middle of nowhere, right?"

"I know, and I love it! I thought I'd miss Rochester and being around people, but I have to say, I'm enjoying the time to myself. Although, I don't always feel like I'm alone." I told Nancy about the feeling of not being alone in the house, and of hearing strange things at night. I did not tell her about the nightmare, though, afraid that I would sound like a nut. I realized then that I was telling the truth about enjoying the time to myself, even though I was creeped out half the time. Something about the house still made me feel safe.

"Old houses definitely have history. Did you do any research before you bought the place?" Nancy asked.

I laughed. "No, of course not! Why would I do a reasonable thing like that? I am actually on my way to the local library now to see what I can dig up."

"No pun intended, I hope! Well, be careful of what you wish for. Sometimes it's probably better not to know," Nancy cautioned. "But if you do find out anything juicy, be sure to let me know."

"I will. Alright, I think I have to turn around. I just drove right through town. God, this place is small," I told her, turning my Jeep Grand Cherokee around at the Mobil gas station.

"Hey, Annabelle?" Nancy got my attention back. "I'm proud of you. And I know that Mom and Dad would be, too."

"Thanks, sis. I hope they are." I was touched, and saddened, to think of my parents. "I really hope so."

We promised to be in touch soon, and I vowed to invite her for a visit when I was ready. I slowed down through town this time, concentrating on my surroundings.

I was happy to explore my new town and found the library off Main Street with ease. The library was quaint and tidy, in an old brick building that looked like it had been around since my house was constructed.

As I walked through the doors, the first thing that I recognized was the smell of the books. It was a scent that I have always loved, more than any bottled perfume. It is like breathing in the smell of a thousand different stories at once. The library was small. I noticed a tiny sign for a kids' section in the basement.

I went straight toward the library assistant, knowing that if I needed any help, it was best to get on their good side. I usually found that smaller libraries did not carry an array of material, sticking to what was asked for the most or studied in school.

I found the library assistant perched behind the desk. A very pretty, young-looking woman with short brown hair and glasses glanced up from her computer.

"Hi, may I help you?" she asked, smiling at me.

I grabbed a pen and pad from my purse and smiled at her. "Yes, thanks. I am doing research on a house in the area that I recently purchased, and thought this was a good place to start."

Her smile faltered, and she looked at me over her glasses. "You want housing information from the library..." she said, posing her question more as a statement.

"Yes, I do, because the house I am researching is pretty old. I thought maybe there was some history there," I explained. I told her my address, and she suddenly looked interested in my quest for information.

"That house is an 1860 farmhouse," she told me, looking up at me with curiosity. "You actually live there?"

"Yes, I bought the house a few months ago, after I left my husband," I answered, cursing myself for telling anyone personal information. One rule I live by is to not give out personal information to strangers. Yet there I was, spilling information that was better kept private.

"You live there alone?" the woman asked me, her big brown eyes widening even more behind her glasses. For a moment, she looked like a college freshman dishing gossip. "I'm sorry, my name is Kelly, and I'm the library assistant here," she said, holding her hand out over the desk.

Not knowing whether I wanted to know more about the house after all and wishing I had done more research before jumping so quickly, I took her hand and was happy to get an actual firm shake. "I'm Annabelle Peterson," I told Kelly, giving my maiden name even though I was technically still a Hayes by marriage. "And yes, happily living alone for the first time since college. But, ah, why do you ask?"

Kelly looked at me a little pensively. "Yours is the house I'm thinking of, right? Down the road from the Anderson farm, across the street from an old pig farm that burned down?"

"Yes—actually, my realtor told me about that. The farm burned down over twenty years ago, though, not exactly a landmark," I answered, a little confused.

"Oh, sorry, yeah, I guess if you're not from here, then you wouldn't even know. It was big news back when it happened—you could smell the burning pigs all the way into town. The crazy thing is," Kelly leaned in and lowered her voice to even lower than the normal library whisper, "bacon sales shot up for weeks after that. Kind of smelled like an outdoor barbecue."

I scrunched up my nose at that, not bothering to tell Kelly that I'm actually a vegetarian. "So other than the famous bacon frenzy, is there anything else you can tell me about the house?" I asked.

Kelly looked over my shoulder and smiled. I followed her gaze, expecting to see someone standing there, but besides the two of us, the room was empty. I looked back at Kelly, who smiled wider before getting up from her desk and walking to the bookshelves behind me. She picked up a soft covered book with a dark blue cover and what looked like a very old, very scary house. The title was *Hauntings of Ontario County, Volume 1*.

"Oh great," I murmured.

"Your house is in here," Kelly said as she handed me the book. "Feel free to take a seat in one of the reading areas and take a look."

I took the book from her, feeling a little sweaty, and closed in. With a quick thank you, I made my way to the rear of the library and found a comfortable old red reading chair in a little nook. As I sat down, I remembered the first time that I experienced what I felt was a spiritual encounter. It was about a year before I decided to see what Wicca was all about, while on a date with a guy that I met while attending a driver's education course at the local technical school. His name was Steve, and he was a terrible kisser. Wet, sloppy. He drove me to an abandoned run-down house in the middle of nowhere, which was a good hour away from the school, and we snuck inside to make out.

Just as I was wondering how to politely convince Steve to wipe his mouth and take me home, a painting fell off the wall. We quietly walked over, shone a light on it, and found ourselves looking at a painting of a smiling old woman who seemed to be looking right at me. We walked to the left, and to the right, and then we each walked in opposite directions, and wherever I went, the woman was looking right at me. It was a portrait that was in sad shape, probably painted in the early 1900s, with some water damage in the corners. It spooked Steve and so we left, but before leaving, I made sure to look the woman in the eyes and whisper *thank you*. When I got home and told Nancy about how the woman in the painting saved me, she just rolled her eyes and told me I was being ridiculous.

It wasn't until months later that I was finally able to learn about spirits and energy, and I soaked up everything I could find on the subject. When I joined a small coven, Nancy flipped out, insisting that belonging to a coven was dangerous, and all they did was have orgies and drink too much. This was soon after my parents' death, so I didn't rub it in her face too much. I practiced in secret, which actually made it feel more special. As older sisters often are, it turned out that she was right about the drinking, and although I practiced more on my own, it really was the coven that put me on the right path.

I leafed through the first few pages, looking through the chapter headlines for something that may have to do with my house. Chapters like "A Sailor's Return," "The Dog Who Came Back," and "The Musician" didn't sound too promising. I flipped through to look at photos, and about halfway through the book came face-to-face with a photo of a very pristine version of my house, and after a moment's hesitation, began to read.

The Hauntings of Ontario County
UNOCCUPIED

This Naples, NY, farmhouse seems like the perfect family home. Lots of land, an apple orchard, fishing pond, and ample space make it seem like a desirable location. There is just one tiny problem—the house itself doesn't seem to want anyone living there.

Most folks don't even make it through the first walk-through with the Realtor before running out and not looking back. Sources who have gone through the house say it's more than just the creepy feeling they get when they walk inside, it's the "jump scare" factor; doors slamming, a corner radio, turning on and off, windows not just closing on their own but opening as well, and the feeling of being pushed while sitting in the kitchen rocking chair.

Tragedy struck first in 1904 with the death of the lady of the house, Mrs. Judith Boyd, then again in 1908, when the daughter, Kelly, died of tuberculosis.

All was quiet at the farmstead until Mr. Charles Boyd died in 1913 of heart disease. Of course, his son insisted his father died of a broken heart.

Once Mr. Boyd had passed, his son, Christian, shut down the farm and made his living using his brain instead of his brawn. A poet and short story novelist, Christian sold an array of his works for publication. His work became deeper and darker when his fiancée left him, however, and sadly, he succumbed to suicide in the fall of 1917.

Since that time, the house has stood empty, except for brief periods of ownership that were short-lived. The house has been bought and sold at least a dozen times over the past ninety-plus years, making it the longest marketed house in the county.

. . .

The story went on to say that, besides scaring folks off with things going bump in the night, people have reported seeing a man in the upstairs bedroom window at night, and those walking by in the daytime have heard sorrowful music drifting from the house. At one point, the Naples Historical Society was looking into buying the house, but withdrew their interest. Various Realtors have kept up the appearance of the house, which keeps getting passed around by various buyers.

I read to the end of the article, goose bumps all over my body, and stopped cold. At the end, right in front of my eyes, was a family photo taken of the Boyd family. It was a typical photo from that era, with the unsmiling family posing in front of the house. There, I recognized Christian, the boy from my dream. But what gave me cold chills up my spine was the mother, looking much more alive than when I had seen her laid out in the parlor of my home, dead and yet reaching out for her screaming son.

Chapter Six

"Sweet dreams till sunbeams find you
Sweet dreams that leave all worries behind you
But in your dreams whatever they be
Dream a little dream of me."
–Louis Armstrong, Count Basie Orchestra, Ella Fitzgerald,
"Dream a Little Dream of Me"

Driving around Naples aimlessly, seeing the country roads and farms but not taking any of it in, I thought over the rest of my research in the library. After I read the piece in *The Hauntings of Ontario County, Volume 1*, I got up and walked around the library until that cold fear resting in my spine subsided a bit. I actually saw a photo of the dead people in my dream.

Up and down roads I had never been on before, I kept repeating to myself, "It wasn't a dream," over and over until I had to stop driving in circles and stick with a direction. As unreal as it seemed, I also realized that I knew it was no ordinary dream. I kept thinking about everything else I had found out at the library.

What intrigued me the most was what I learned about Christian. I was convinced that he was the spirit haunting my house, and from what I read about the house being uninhabitable because of paranormal activity, I thought I was lucky that my experience has been pretty mild by comparison. The thing is, knowing that I am not crazy and imagining things made me feel better. And somehow, knowing that Christian was a poet and a storyteller made me feel a sort of kinship with him, and I felt sad when I learned that he had killed himself. I grew up writing poems myself. Whenever I have a big emotion that I can't explain, I turn to poetry to help me work through it. This was actually one of the problems with Scott and me, as I have been in search of a deeper meaning in life, and his depth consisted of baseball games and wearing the newest styles. That was not the only problem between us, of course. When I first met him, he was charming and caring, always ready to make me laugh or dream up some fancy way to show that he loved me. That turned into something different once we were married. Possessive, narcissistic, with a volatile temper, Scott had disappointed me at every turn. He also liked to build himself up by making me look bad in front of other people, yelling at me or calling me stupid. Of course, there was also the pushing and occasional hitting, but with a little distance between us, I realized it was the emotional abuse that hurt me the most.

As I got lost in thought and memories, I realized that I had driven outside of town and had reached Canandaigua Lake, a vast expanse that opened up the surrounding sky. I pushed the memories of Scott from my mind and thought more about my house. My home. And about how I could stay there without living in fear of being haunted. My days of contacting spirits and seeking the thrill of a good ghost story were behind me—or so I thought— and I had no desire to battle with a ghost.

Even though I experienced everything in that house from being scared out of my wits to being pissed off that I wasn't allowed peace in my own home to being slightly wary every time the sun dipped down for the night and I knew that many long hours of darkness lay ahead, I still felt as though I were home, that I was meant to be here.

Needing a bit more distance to digest all the information that I had found, I decided on a whim to head back into town and see what Aunt Lizzy's coffee shop was all about. After heading my car back toward Main Street and finding a place to park—which was not too difficult in such a small town—I opened the door to the shop and was immediately consumed by the delicious scent of coffee, mixed with a light patchouli and vanilla. I spotted Lizzy right away, working behind the counter and chatting happily with her customers.

Lizzy saw me and made her way over. As I glanced around at the decor, which was bohemian and instantly relaxing, Lizzy brought me a menu. Because of her free-spirited persona, it did not surprise me to see that the menu she handed me was handwritten on heavy paper. I could imagine her with a feather and ink, sketching out a cup and a pastry on each personalized menu.

"It's great to see you, honey! I was hoping you'd stop by for the reading."

I had forgotten about the poetry reading, and my stomach tightened at the thought of reading in public. "Reading? Oh right, I was really just in the neighborhood and wanted to say hello."

"Well, you've got a good hour until it starts, but we'd love for you to stay. It's always a treat when a real writer does a reading," Lizzy told me.

I was confused, and asked, "A real writer?"

"Oh honey, you didn't think that I wouldn't have recognized your name right away, did you?" Lizzy looked at me hopefully. "I'd love for you to read a poem. You do write poetry, don't you? I had read that in your bio once. When I got home after meeting you the other day, I knew I recognized your name, and so I Googled you. I have friends that live near Rochester, and they always love your stories and columns in the *Gazette*."

I was surprised, and a little honored. Writing about community events wasn't exactly big time in the newspaper business. I was a little sorry that I had included that I like to write poetry in my bio, though, because while I wrote it, I also didn't necessarily love reading it out loud. I have always been shy about expressing my feelings. Part of me wanted to make up an excuse and leave, but another part of me wanted to stay. I felt like something inside of me was changing. I did the thing that I had been most afraid of: I left my husband. I put myself first and summoned every ounce of courage that I had to do that, and I liked that part of myself. I felt myself stand a little taller that night and decided to keep taking chances.

I smiled at my new friend, feeling grateful. "I didn't bring anything to read, but if you have a pencil and paper handy, I have been toying with something in my head that I could probably work out in the next hour." Since I was young, I had a knack for thinking about a poem or a rhyme for days on end and being able to take it from my mind to the paper in just minutes if I made myself concentrate.

As Lizzy showed me to a table in the corner next to a tapestry covered in elephants and some very peaceful-smelling incense, I asked her about the stories that her mom had told her about the house.

"Oh, I'm sorry I said anything. It was just a little unnerving, being right at your front door, after speculating for so long. I'm sure it's just stories," Lizzy told me.

I gave Lizzy a quick rundown of what I learned in the library, leaving out my dream and the feeling of being watched in the house. Lizzy listened as though this history was not news to her.

"To be honest with you," Lizzy said, her voice dropping to a whisper, "I already knew that there was a young man who killed himself in the barn on the property. He was heartbroken over a nasty breakup with his fiancée and hung himself. The house has seemed to want to remain empty since that day, and my mom had told me she used to hear a sorrowful cry coming from inside." As she spoke, I felt a chill crawling up my back like tentacles, brushing my skin in a careless caress.

"And I'm guessing that is why you said something about the house letting me stay?" I asked her, fighting off a mild annoyance at the secrets.

Lizzy looked more than sufficiently shamed. "I suffer from foot in mouth syndrome," she said, looking worried but covering it with a shrug and a smile. I let her off the hook, realizing that if I knew a house was haunted, I would have no idea how to go about telling the new resident that fact. Honestly, I probably wouldn't have had the guts to even knock on the door to say hello, so I gave Lizzy credit for reaching out.

The house didn't seem to want to remain empty to me, not at all. To me, it seemed like the house—or someone in the house— had something to say. There was a connection to be made there. I just knew it.

A commotion in the kitchen startled me out of my revelation. The clanking of dishes reverberated off the walls of the small shop. Lizzy ran off to see what was happening, leaving me to finish my poem—which ironically was about the very story that I was just told, a poem that was starting to make sense, a fact that was not reassuring at all.

About an hour later, full of too much coffee and sticky buns, which Lizzy brought over to me herself after cleaning up the "mild disaster" in the kitchen, I sat listening to surprisingly good poetry from a few locals. When it was my turn, Lizzy made a big production of announcing me, which was embarrassing because I never thought that my poetry was very good. With a very humble thanks to Lizzy, I stood at the makeshift podium and began to read. "I titled this poem *Whose Memories*."

> *Whose eyes do I see through as I walk these rooms —*
> *Through whose nose do I smell the scent of percolated coffee?*
> *What memory do I remember that is not mine, seen through a haze yet clear as day.*
> *This house—my home — is awake now.*
> *I close my eyes and see hands — my hands?— tying a noose, wiping a tear,*
> *I feel my breathing restrict,*
> *I know my heart will burst.*
> *Whose memories do I see, as I hang from a wooden beam?*
> *They are not mine.*
> *Yet they come from within.*
> *To whom do they belong?*

I stayed at the poetry reading until it was over, meeting new people and having more fun than I could remember in quite a long time. I liked this new Annabelle. I hadn't felt so strong or sure of myself in a long time. The smell of the freshly brewed coffee and the sound of the words read by the people in this small town were intoxicating. I felt like I was at home. As I finished my cup and looked around the room, I felt like I was looking around with new eyes.

Lizzy knew everyone, and introduced me to people like Sam and Theresa, the owners of the diner down the road, who seemed to never take their eyes off each other all night. There was Betty, a retired middle school teacher with a shiny gray bob and milky brown eyes. She read a poem about school violence that brought tears to my eyes. A man named Ben stood to read at one point, but when he pulled a worn-looking piece of folded-up paper from his back pocket and looked around the room, he gave a shy apology and sat back down. When Lizzy introduced me to Ben, who owns the Grapes of Wrath Winery on the outskirt of town, she actually waggled her eyes at me as she turned to cash out another customer. Handsome as he was—and he was definitely handsome in his torn jeans and Birkenstocks—tall with dark messy hair and bright blue eyes, I just wasn't interested in romance at the time. After a few minutes of chatting with him, I realized that I recognized him from a tour of the winery that I had done a few years back with Nancy, on one of her rare visits to upstate New York. It was actually the memory of that trip that made me choose Naples as my new home. The town had a friendly, old-fashioned feel to it, and I remembered feeling safe.

I lingered at the shop until Lizzy closed up for the night. As I drove home, I felt good about my future as a member of this town, and felt that ghost or no ghost, I would be able to handle whatever came my way.

That night was uneventful, perhaps a bit too quiet, and I cleaned my way through the hours.

Once I was satisfied that I had put my energy into each and every corner of the house, I poured myself a glass of Vine Valley raspberry wine, my favorite new local wine, grabbed some materials that I checked out of the library, and sat down on my bed. I had lots of material to go through and fanned it all out over the bed. I started with photos of the house in the early days, with Christian's family gathered for a photo in the front yard being among the best ones, but the hardest for me to look at. Chills ran down my spine when I looked at the mother, alive and vibrant, surrounded by her family, looking directly at the camera. I kept looking over my shoulder, as if I were hiding my research. I had piles of papers and articles, including Christian's obituary, which of course did not say that he killed himself. My best find, though, was a poem that Christian himself had written—a poem that I could only guess was written soon before he committed suicide. It was found in his bedroom after he died and later published in the town's historical anthology. The poem broke my heart. It read:

My heart is mortally wounded.
It is outside of my body split open on the hard, wooden floor.
Without you there is no I— no reason for my lungs to take in air.
No reason for my broken heart to beat again.
My blood pumps loneliness.
I am dead already.
—Christian Boyd, 1917

By the time the clock ticked on midnight, there were papers and books spread out all over the bed, some falling onto the floor, and I slept soundly in the center of the mess.

While I slept, I met Christian for the first time.

• • •

It was raining as I came out of the woods and walked toward the house. I was happy to see that there was smoke coming from the chimney because that meant warmth was waiting for me when I stepped inside. I opened the front door leading into the kitchen and noticed that the door did not stick as it usually did.

I knew I was dreaming without really thinking about it. My hair was already dry, as were my clothes. A glass of red wine was ready at the kitchen table, served in a vintage etched wineglass. The house looked different: the walls were dingy, the cabinets were their original unpainted wood, and all of my personal touches were missing.

Sensing I was not alone, yet unafraid, I closed my eyes. I took a few deep breaths. When I opened them there was a man sitting across the table from me. He wore slim-fitting black pants, a plain white pullover shirt, and long black boots. I smiled and asked, "Christian?"

Christian sat perfectly still.

He did not move. Eyes wide and looking at me, he was as motionless as a statue. He seemed shocked that I was there with him. He was very real, sitting at the table, sandy blond hair dipping into his eyes. For a ghost, he sure seemed solid.

"Christian, it's okay. My name is Annabelle, and I've been hoping to meet you," I said. I did not dare reach out for his hand. "You have a beautiful home."

"Home," he said, sounding out the word slowly. "Yes, it is." Christian gave me a sad smile in return.

Looking around the room for a moment, I picked up the wineglass and took a sip. "Thank you for the wine," I told him, to which he nodded politely.

Christian was sitting coolly at the other side of the table, looking uncomfortable. Although I knew that this was the spirit who had been haunting me, I felt sad for him. He hadn't harmed me, yet he had definitely given me a good scare. I looked at his neck and he instantly put his hand on his throat.

"Christian." I leaned toward him a bit, speaking softly. "I'm sorry for what happened to you."

Christian shrugged, looking more like the child in my dream than a grown man. "What I did to me, I suppose," he answered, leaning closer as well, dark brown eyes looking straight into mine. "Why are you here, Annabelle?"

The question took me by surprise. "Well, I needed a change in my life, and from the second I saw this house listed for sale, I just fell in love with it," I told him honestly.

Christian nodded. "But why have you stayed?" It was more of a whisper than a question.

"You mean, why haven't you scared me off?" I smiled and took another sip of my wine. "Because being here, in your house, with your spirit going bump in the night, is nothing compared to what I have been through."

"Your husband..." Christian asked hesitantly, "Did you leave him for another man?" It took me a moment to realize that he was privy to my private life.

The sorrow that surrounded his question made me want to reach out to him. It was sorrow that I had felt myself. "No, Christian, I never would have done that." Instead of trying to explain what it was like to be married to a man like Scott, I simply pulled down the neck of my own sweater, so that my collarbone was exposed. I knew that he would see a dent in my bone, badly healed from a fracture. Christian reached out to touch it but pulled his hand away just as his fingers were about to make contact.

"Annabelle," he whispered, a single tear falling down one cheek.

I reached out to take his hand, but grabbed only a fistful of bedsheet. Suddenly very awake, I touched my face and realized I had been crying in my sleep. As the dream came back to me, I got up out of bed and went into the kitchen for some water. Looking at my reflection in the window over the sink, I told myself that I had to ease up on the obsession about the house. I was a mess, hair tangled in knots and bags under my eyes. Peering closer into the window at my reflection, I noticed the kitchen table behind me.

Spinning around, heart kicking back into high gear, I walked slowly over and sat down in the spot where I was sitting in my dream. In front of me was a very dusty antique glass. The glass was empty, yet carried the distinct odor of my favorite wine.

Chapter Seven

"When I discover who I am, I'll be free."
-Ralph Ellison, *Invisible Man*

"An ye harm none, do as ye will." Words from my past kept coming back to me as my dream went from an occurrence to a memory. As the days ticked by, and the leaves began to change from green to red and orange around me, many of them scattering over the fallen apples on the ground, I noticed the quiet everywhere. Outside, while taking a walk, the freshly fallen leaves cushioned each step. Inside the house, the quiet was almost unbearable, as I looked for signs of Christian and found none. Not a door slam or a window suddenly flying open, and I found myself surprisingly disappointed in my meaningless dreams.

My column deadline was already overdue, yet I couldn't find it in myself to focus. I would sit down, fully intending to work, and moments later I'd catch myself staring into space, or rereading Christian's poem, or playing solitaire on my computer. Frequently, I would remember my younger years when I practiced Wicca. Witchcraft always made me feel powerful and, always sticking to the harm none rule, I felt like I was making positive changes in my life.

I dropped the practice altogether when I met Scott. He said that it freaked him out, and I was so eager to please that I figured it was time to "grow up,"—which was actually his words. Looking back, I can see that he was afraid of the independence that I felt when I was practicing because I did it solo and I excluded him. Even a simple house protection ritual to make me feel safe in our new condo threw him over the edge.

The Wiccan Rede—*An ye harm none, do as ye will*—made me think of Christian and his suicide. I had once believed that suicide was morally wrong because it went against the council of the religion that got me through hard times, just as the concept of harming none, including harming oneself, stopped me from considering the possibility of taking my own life at one low point. But so much had changed since I was that person, so much heartache and physical pain, I could no longer say with any certainty what was right and what was wrong. I wondered, if we are all responsible for our own lives, isn't it our sole decision to end it?

The wind was kicking up the leaves that fell, and I decided to take a walk down the street to visit Lizzy. I walked slowly, methodically, trying to take my mind off Christian's sad brown eyes and images of him hanging from the barn, images that I didn't know if I conjured into my mind myself or if I had somehow gained the knowledge through some connection that I had with him. I took a few deep breaths, basking in the warm sun and the scent of fall. I don't know how anyone can live in a place where they cannot smell the seasons change. It took only about five minutes to walk to my new friend's house, but it was enough to start to clear my mind a bit.

Lizzy's house had a large celestial door knocker, with the sun painted yellow and the moon a deep orange. She answered on the first knock. "Oh Annabelle, I am so glad to see you," she said, welcoming me inside right away. As she shut the door behind me, I noticed her look in the direction of my house.

Her home was very much like the coffee shop, with tapestries on the walls and incense in the air. The thick scent of honey almond hung in the air. "I'm sorry to come by without calling, but I just needed to chat with someone. It is so quiet here this time of year," I told her.

"Oh, that's no problem, honey. Although to be honest, it's quiet here every time of the year," Lizzy told me while putting on a pot of tea, which I smiled about, seeing as how Lizzy owned a coffee shop. "I was just getting ready to head to the shop, but I have time. And yes, it sure must be different from living in Rochester. Sometimes, when the wind is still and the coyotes are keeping their mouths shut, I swear I can hear the mice farting. Of course, *your* particular house is not exactly known as a peaceful retreat for guests."

I laughed at the image and rolled my eyes when Lizzy nodded toward my house. "I think I have had my fill of ghost stories for a while. After I got home from the poetry reading, I had the most realistic dream about Christian. And now I just feel like my mind made all of this up, maybe to distract me from my divorce. There is nothing like a good ghost story to distract yourself from the fact that your husband is trying to find you and won't sign papers." I took the steaming cup of pumpkin spice tea from Lizzy. Inhaling the steam, I told my friend, "It all just seemed so real."

I told Lizzy about my most recent dream, minus the detail about the wineglass, as that was something I wanted to keep to myself. Talking about a strange dream was one thing, but admitting out loud that my house may or may not be haunted—really, truly, I live with a ghost haunted - and that I may or may not actually be talking to a ghost in my dreams, who may or may not have *actually* served me wine at the kitchen table, was something that I thought might challenge our new friendship.

"You know, my mother was five years old when that young man hung himself and, while she didn't remember any details, she did remember that he was kind to her. She supposed that he was the kind of man that was too deep into his emotions, who felt too much. I have lived down the road from that house for most of my life, and I have never once felt scared. Sad maybe, and curious as all heck of course, but never afraid." Lizzy touched my arm. It was a warm gesture that I had missed. "And if he is haunting the place, maybe he's just looking for a connection." Lizzy smiled and polished off her pumpkin spice tea. "And if it is all in your head, well, it will make a great story one day!" I laughed and nodded my head. "Yes, I suppose it will," I said.

Lizzy was quiet for a minute, and I knew before she opened her mouth that she was going to ask me about Scott. I felt a sense of dread. I didn't want to talk about Scott. I didn't want to think about Scott. Lizzy stood and walked over to her kitchen counter, rubbing her hand lightly over the mosaic sunflower pattern. She carefully struck a match and lit some sage. As the smoke bellowed toward me, I had to suppress the urge to cough.

As Lizzy put the bundle down, she asked me the dreaded question. "What's your story, Annabelle? I feel like we are old friends already, yet I don't even know why you've moved into a big old farmhouse, all alone. You mentioned that your husband is trying to find you and won't sign anything. Divorce papers, I'm assuming?"

The way she looked at me diffused any annoyance I may have had at the question. Her eyes were all kindness as she quietly waited for my answer.

I took a sip of tea and put down my cup, splashing the hot tea over the shaking rim.

"Never mind," she said, and reached out to steady my hand. "I don't need to know anything."

"No, it's okay," I said as I mopped up my mess with a napkin that was thankfully on the table. "I don't know why I feel so ashamed. Lots of women are abused, lots of woman are just like me and they always feel ashamed and guilty. That was me—a dumb girl who tried to be a perfect wife and do everything right until I realized that I could do nothing right. Nothing was good enough for him." I realized I was babbling and took a few deep breaths to stop myself. I closed my eyes and the words I have been shamefully holding in spit right out. "I fell in love and married a man who was kind and gentle and fun. As soon as I found a little independence, after what I call our honeymoon period ended, he became jealous and possessive, and he would yell and scream at me for nothing. He berated me for things out of my control, like if his clothes suddenly fit too tight, saying that I must have shrunk them and that I was purposely trying to make him feel bad. He embarrassed me in front of my friends, and eventually his anger left his mouth and came through his fists."

I pulled down the neck of my sweater and showed Lizzy the scar. "He did this after he caught me on the phone with a man one night. That man was my seventy-one-year-old editor, and I was discussing a story idea. I thought he might kill me." I paused, realizing that tears had started to fall. I angrily wiped them away. "I had enough. And so, I left."

I was not completely honest with Lizzy. In this version of my story, I would not let my husband treat me like he did and so I left. In reality, it took me way too long, and I made excuse after excuse to stay with him. I blamed myself for so long, thinking that I had done something wrong and deserved the abuse. It was not strength that drove me to leave. That came later. It was fear, exhaustion, and a tiny spark of hope that I deserved better than I was getting. The strength came as I was driving away, and while I was moving into the house. It crept into my bones in the dark hours of the night as I realized that I was stronger without him.

To my surprise, when I was done with my story, I felt good. I did not feel ashamed, and when I looked at Lizzy, I knew that I had done the right thing. She was a strong woman, and so was I.

Lizzy said nothing as she came around the table and pulled me to my feet. She hugged me tight to her, and when she let me go, she smiled and said, "Fuck that creep you married."

I laughed. It was just what I needed. The burning sage was no longer bothering my throat, and I took a deep breath in. That was the first time I had shared my story with anyone, and I felt very strong. Brave. I also felt a little guilty because I knew that I should have shared that story with Nancy.

Needing to lighten the conversation, I asked Lizzy if she had ever left Naples, and she sucked me in with a story of a donkey, a small-town circus, a fat lady, a skinny man, a few dozen well-trained chickens, and the love of her life, Juan. As Lizzy told the story, I laughed until my stomach was sore. I wasn't sure if the story was true or not, but thought it might be when I asked Lizzy what her role in this circus was and she looked at me quite seriously and answered, "The fortune-teller, of course. 'The Great Liz Beth, Oracle of the People!'" Lizzy spread her arms wide and puffed out her chest, winking at me.

"Well, I guess that's how you knew we'd be friends," I told Lizzy, hugging her and drying my eyes from laughter-induced streaks.

We decided to exchange phone numbers, since we were close neighbors and friends. It was a weird feeling, comforting in a way that I had forgotten. I had a friend, one that I could visit just by walking down the street. I had a feeling that things were falling into place for me.

Suddenly, I wanted to go back to the house. Saying goodbye, and in much better spirits, I walked home. I felt good, and decided that to celebrate my independence, I was going to commemorate the fall equinox.

As I opened the door to my kitchen and focused on the task of making a list of supplies that I would need—some wine and cheese, a few candles, some altar items—I didn't even notice at first that all of my kitchen windows were wide open, and the radio softly played John McCormack's "Send Me Away with a Smile," which I later learned was a top-playing song in 1917. A little breeze blew through the window, and when I felt it, my writing stopped, and goose bumps traveled up my back. The sudden change in energy around me was chilling. I heard a sound that resembled the inhale of breath, like someone was right by my side, breathing me in. That was when I heard the music and noticed the windows.

As the shock wore off and my heartbeat returned to normal, I felt desperate for a connection with the spirit in my home.

"Christian?" I whispered his name, hearing nothing in return, only the soft music playing.

Repeating the lyrics to the song on the radio, I softly sang, "*Little girl, don't cry. I must say goodbye.*" I smiled, and hummed the tune I did not know while moving around the kitchen to close the windows. Picking my notepad and pen back up to finish my list, I knew that I was not alone, yet I also knew that Christian could not reach me in that moment. I had a feeling that if not for my dreams, he wouldn't be able to reach me at all.

As I put the shopping list into my purse, ready to go out for supplies and some food for the night, I felt a breeze pass through me, even though I had shut the windows that had mysteriously been opened. I stopped moving and noticed that the radio was again turned off, and the only sound in the house was the ticking of the kitchen clock.

"Christian?" I whispered again, touching my arm, and again feeling goose bumps on my skin. There was no sound in return, no hint of a whisper, nothing but the sound of the clock, counting down the minutes that I had yet to learn were becoming so precious to him.

Chapter Eight

*"Sunflowers end up facing the sun, but they go through
a lot of dirt to find their way there."*
–J.R. Rim

The room was perfect. Although I had at one time belonged to a small coven, I had always preferred to practice on my own. Being in a coven felt strange—fake—like we were gathering more to hang by a bonfire and make music. I was a young adult when I joined and always felt like an imposter. Once I decided to practice as a solitary witch, the practice was more grounding for me.

I decorated my favorite room in the house, the kitchen, in all fall colors. The kitchen table had an orange silk runner with a vase of freshly cut sunflowers in the center, surrounded by tiny pumpkins. The fireplace was lit and smelled wonderful, and as the sun went down, throwing shades of orange and red through the windows, I felt more content than I had in years.

I set an altar on a small table near the fireplace. I used a small set of scales as a symbol of that balance, a simple pair of white and black candles, and a yin-yang symbol on a silver tray. Also on the altar was a small statue of Ganesh, the elephant-headed deity who was worshipped as the remover of obstacles and patron of learning.

I watched the sunset through the kitchen window while I poured myself a glass of red wine, which wouldn't be sipped until my rituals were finished. Known as the pagan Thanksgiving,

Mabon marks the Autumn Equinox, when day and night are equal. This is a time of harmony and balance. While there are often festivals or large gatherings to celebrate, it is also acceptable to celebrate on your own. I planned on starting with a Mabon Meditation before holding a ceremony to honor the Dark Mother, the Crone aspect of the triple goddess. The meditation I used that night was one that I had written myself, years ago. Although I had not done this since I met Scott, it was still in my memory. I lit the two candles, sat on a cushion in front of the warm fireplace, and closed my eyes, repeating the meditation:

There is balance all around me starting with the dark sky and circling to the light.

Day and night in harmony making everything feel right.

I cleanse my soul with candles, rising smoke lifts the darkness inside of me, while a white light of protection and love settles into my soul and sets me free.

Thank you, Dark Mother, for your wisdom, guidance, and love.

I can feel you all around me, as below, so above.

Harmony and balance on this day and through the seasons, please keep this message in my heart and make me remember the reasons.

May we never forget this message of equality, of dark and light, day, and night, death, life, and morality.

For a few minutes, with eyes still closed, I felt totally relaxed and in touch with the energies around me. My mind wandered to the house, and then to Christian. I imagined he was with me in the kitchen, maybe moving around the room, watching me sitting near the candles, maybe even reaching out to touch me. I imagined him sitting next to me, holding my hand. I was so engrossed in thought that when the pounding started on the kitchen door, I jumped up with a yell, noticing right away that the candles around me all went out with an invisible wind.

I went to the door and flicked on the outside light, sucking in my breath when I saw the face of my husband. "Scott," I whispered, as my fingers trembled. For a moment I wondered if I had summoned him here with my magic, but knew right away that this was just a coincidence, or maybe even pure bad luck that I was reentering the world of witchcraft, something that I used to love, and for a few minutes had let my guard down.

I did not open the door. "Scott, what are you doing here?" I asked through the glass window.

"That's how you greet your husband?" Scott smiled at me and opened his arms in a welcoming gesture.

Even through the glass of the window, I could see that his eyes were bloodshot, a sure sign that he had been drinking. I stood my ground and wrapped my arms around myself. "Go away, Scott, I am not letting you in."

Scott's smile disappeared in an instant. "Of course you will," he told me. "I want to talk to you, that's all." And then, the desperate "please" that I had heard too many times.

I looked down at the doorknob and realized that I had not locked it, a mistake I found myself making more often as I started to feel comfortable in my environment. Scott saw me looking, too, and before I could reach the handle, he had twisted the knob and immediately pushed the door open, shouldering his way through when it stuck.

"Seriously, Scott, this is not okay," I told him, and tried to put as much distance between us as I could, walking to the other side of the kitchen table.

"No, Annabelle, what is not okay is you not returning my calls, is you leaving me and thinking that you can live here in the middle of nowhere and be safe without me, is you thinking that your magic will make you happy." Scott was looking at the altar, disgusted. He pointed his finger at me, narrowing his eyes. "You do not deserve any of this."

"I don't deserve this?" I asked him, feeling defensive and afraid. "And what do I deserve, Scott? A life sentence of being your wife, just because you say so? Of being afraid of saying the wrong thing, walking on eggshells? We have been over for a while and you know it."

Almost as quickly as his anger had appeared at the door, it was seemingly gone. Scott sat at the kitchen table and put his head in his hands. "I don't know what to do without you, Annabelle. I need you. I need you to come home." He tried to reach out to take my hand, but I backed farther away. As much as I had started to hate him, a part of me felt so sad watching him sit there like he was broken. I had heard this speech before, and I knew all too well that if I did not comply and rush to his side, he would open up the verbal thrashing. Still, seeing him sitting there reminded me of a little child, and although wary, I sat down next to him.

"I'm sorry, Scott, but I can't keep on doing this," I told him. "Please, just sign the papers so that we can move on."

"But I don't want to move on," he told me, looking around my kitchen. He seemed like he was looking for something. "Plus, you have something of mine, which tells me that, while you keep saying that you don't want to be with me, you aren't being completely honest with yourself. You, keeping something of mine, tells me that you want to be pursued, that you want me to track you down and beg you to come home with me." He smiled, like he just won an argument. "So here I am, Annabelle, giving you what you want."

I couldn't help it—I laughed at him. This was, I realized, the reason I left him. Yes, he hit me and scared the shit out of me, but it was this—this crazy making, turning everything that I did or said into something that fit into his version of how he wanted things to go. "I have nothing of yours," I told him.

"Oh, yes, you do. You have my mother's painting. You know how valuable that is to me."

"Um, no. It is not yours. She gave it to me, and it is not valuable to you because your mother painted it, it is valuable because its value shot up when she died." I hated to be cruel, but it was the truth. His mom was a struggling artist who was sadly discovered only months before she passed. I was annoyed and pushed from the table to put some distance between us. I felt like an idiot for feeling sorry for him—again.

Scott looked up at me, anger replacing sadness just as quickly as the sadness had replaced the anger. He got up, shoving the entire table aside, knocking the vase of sunflowers to the floor, water spilling over the table and onto my bare feet. He was in front of me in a flash, anger turning his face red as he grabbed my shoulders and shook me. "You are my wife. You belong with me!"

As I tried to back away, Scott grabbed a fistful of my hair and pulled me toward him. He tried to kiss me, and repulsed, I kneed him in the crotch, pushing him back and turning out of his grasp. Scott doubled over for a moment before shoving me, hard, into the counter and kitchen sink.

We have had some major arguments before, but this felt different; more dangerous. No longer feeling anything but fear, I crouched down to the floor, but Scott lifted me by the neck, back up to my feet. He grabbed at my breasts and my backside.

"It's time for you to be a good wife again," he told me, face close to my own.

Every ounce of my being was repulsed. He was stronger than me, and yet I was so disgusted by his touch that I had to fight back. I was afraid, for I had seen this side of him before.

I landed a decent right hook to the side of his head, but Scott barely seemed to notice. He slapped me, and I fell to the floor, smacking my head as I landed. Horrified, but unable to hang on to any coherent thought or movement, I saw Scott smile as I felt myself drifting out of consciousness and watched as he unbuckled his belt.

I was so afraid, my body went numb, and I tried to hold on to consciousness as I felt something breeze past my body. The windows suddenly flew open, the radio blasted static at high volume, and the smoke detector blared. As Scott worked at his zipper, he was thrown across the room by a force that neither one of us could see. Every light in the house went out, while every candle lit at once. It felt like a hurricane force swept through the kitchen.

Scott could only crawl to the door to get himself out of the house. As he lifted himself up and out the door, I felt myself fading. The last thing I remember was the kitchen door shutting, and as it did, the smoke detector went quiet, the windows went back down, and the radio again softly played tunes of the early 1900s.

Chapter Nine

"All that we see or seem is but a dream within a dream."
–Edgar Allan Poe

When I was an undergraduate student studying creative writing and journalism at the University of Rochester, I was given an assignment to write a scene describing my worst fear. My piece was flagged by my professor and chosen to be a published piece in the student journal, but when Dr. Savale called me into her office to let me know I was selected for this honor, I declined. I did not want to share my fear with others, to discuss it or even worse, be praised for my articulateness in describing something so awful. Rape was not something that I wanted to represent in any format, and had I known that others would read what I had written, I would have chosen a different fear to write about.

I woke up screaming. It was so loud and piercing that I frightened myself, not sure where the sound was coming from. The scream seemed to bounce off the walls. I couldn't remember what had happened exactly, or what the outcome was, but all I could immediately recall was Scott going for his pants, and me feeling helpless and afraid. It wasn't until I heard the soft music playing that I realized I was okay.

Still lying on the floor, I closed my eyes and very softly sang along: *"When I leave you, dear, give me words of cheer to recall in times of pain. They will comfort me and will seem to be like the sunshine after the rain."*

I felt a cold washcloth over my eyes and smiled for a second. Then I realized I was not alone. I grabbed the cloth, opened my eyes, and sat up, sucking in a breath as I saw Christian standing in front of me. Holding out his hand, I reached out my own and tentatively let our fingers touch. It was a solid touch, and Christian closed his eyes in what looked like pleasure. The words that came to mind then were that he swooned. I let him help me up, and with one hand holding his, I used my other hand to support myself on the counter. I was afraid to break contact.

"Am I dreaming?" I softly asked.

Christian smiled at me, still holding my hand in his own. "You are, I think. You bumped your head," he said, touching my head with his free hand. "Here, sit." He led me to the kitchen table, which was in place and undisturbed, vase of flowers in the center.

I sat down but did not let go of his hand, and Christian sat beside me.

The altar candles were burning, as well as several candles that I had set up as decorations. The logs in the fireplace threw off enough warmth so that I felt flushed. I found that the wine that I had set aside for after my ritual was on the table, but was again in the same vintage glass as when I last had a dream with Christian.

"If I am dreaming," I asked, "is this real?"

Christian brought the fingers of his free hand to my face and lightly stroked my cheek. "It is real, I think. I've never done this before," he told me.

I looked around at the kitchen. It was just as I had it set up before Scott interrupted my ritual. "What happened? Where is Scott?" I asked him. "Did you save me?"

Christian told me he was there when I was doing the meditation. "I was right in front of you. I thought maybe you could see me. I wanted to reach out and touch you. And then *he* came here, and oh, Annabelle..." Christian was getting upset and angry all over again. "I thought he might kill you."

"But he's gone now," I said, taking both of Christian's hands in my own. "How?"

Christian closed his eyes, and when he opened them, he looked directly into mine. He smiled, and said, "I felt stronger than I ever have, even when I was alive. When I saw what he was doing to you, and understood what he wanted to do to you, I felt my energy field explode, and I shoved him, throwing him across the room." He squeezed my hands, continuing, "And the rest, well, that was my normal course of haunting when I really did not want someone in the house."

He laughed softly, and I thought I had never met a better person in all of my life. Another song came on the radio, "I Passed By Your Window" by Walter Glynne, and I stood up and pulled Christian to his feet and into my arms. So slowly that we were barely moving, we danced.

I passed by your window in the cool of the night
The lilies were watching so still and so white...

I stopped moving and looked into his eyes.

And though I sang softly
Though no one could hear
To bid you good morning
Good morning, my dear...

The kitchen clock did not keep time during this dream, but if it had, a second would have seemed like an eternity. I felt like I had been holding my breath since we began to dance. I felt so happy and light that I thought I might float away. There was nothing grounding me to the earth, except for the feel of Christian's hand on my lower back. I did not mean to stop dancing with him, I just did. Keeping my eyes wide open, not to miss a second of seeing his face, I stepped forward and closed the small gap between us, and lightly let my lips meet his.

I closed my eyes for just a moment, and as soon as I did, I felt Christian back away. I immediately opened my eyes, but it was too late. I was left back on the floor in the kitchen, in an awkward embrace with myself, longing for a man who I was not quite sure was real.

Chapter Ten

I felt you - cool but solid.
My own heart beating double time while yours remained silent.
I felt you - your hand against my back.
My own steps making sound on the hardwood floor while yours
remained silent.
I felt you - lips against mine.
My own lips letting a sound of pleasure pass through while yours
remained silent.
I felt you - so gently moving from our embrace.
My own cry to ask where you'd gone while you remain silent.

–Annabelle Peterson, 2016

The next morning, I had a lump on the side of my head where I hit the counter, and a terrible headache. I moved around my house slowly, cautiously, and was completely on edge. I seemed to live in extremes: I was either jumpy and worried that Scott would show back up, or I was daydreaming about Christian. I was pretty sure that he saved my life, or at least saved me from being raped. Every time I thought about it, I would cringe at what could have happened. And then he saved me.

Figuring out how Scott found out where I lived was easy. Only a few people knew where I had moved to—my realtor, Nancy, Kelly, from the library, Lizzy, and my editor, Bob. The powers of deduction told me that Scott had gotten to my editor, and I needed to call him to verify, even though I cringed at the thought of calling him when I was pretty sure he was mad at me for being so late.

Of course, he answered on the first ring. "Bob here," he stated, which was the only way I had ever heard him answer the phone.

"Hey Bob, it's your favorite wayward freelancer," I greeted him with a smile, even though he couldn't see it. I hoped that he could sense my good-will toward him and forgive me.

"Annabelle. I was about to filing a missing person's report on you," he said, and I was not one hundred percent sure if he was joking or not.

"I know I've been out of touch, I'm sorry," I told him, not wanting to tell him any details of my very odd personal situation. There is nothing like *anything* out of the ordinary to perk up the attention of a newspaper editor. If I breathed the word ghost, I'm sure that he would have a team of ghost hunters, along with some fresh-out-of-college journalist, on my front door within the hour. "I've sort of been going through a lot," was the only explanation I hoped to give.

It was. "Yes, I figured as much, the way that husband of yours was frantically looking for you. He came here the other day looking for you and had us all worried, saying that he couldn't get in touch with you."

Mystery solved.

"So you gave him my address? Did you, by any chance, remember that I left him? He should be my ex-husband by now," I reminded Bob. For a guy that was such a stickler for facts, he could be so flighty.

"Ah, shit, Annabelle. I'm sorry. He just seemed so worried. I was going to call and let you know he was looking for you, but time just got away from me. So many deadlines these days." That was Bob's apology, and I was going to have to accept it. I also knew that if I checked in with him from time to time, he'd be more apt to do the same. Not to mention that he had no idea that Scott abused me. He just thought that I had enough of married life and decided to call it quits.

"It's alright. Just if anyone else comes looking," I said, knowing that there was no one else, "let human resources handle the inquiry." I knew that Betty in HR would never dream of giving out a personal address. Which is why Scott went to Bob, I was sure.

The call wasn't a total bust, as Bob must have felt guilty enough about giving Scott my address to give me an extension on my story deadline. It was only an extra week, but I took it. He also reminded me that since I choose to become a freelancer, the paper was no longer under any obligation to run my columns. So much for feeling bad, I thought.

For the next few days after the confrontation with Scott, and then the amazing dreamlike kiss with Christian, I looked for signs of Christian everywhere and found nothing. I had not heard from Scott since that night either, which made me wonder what exactly happened while I was passed out. I did, however, contact my attorney and told her that he tried to assault me. Although I decided not to call the cops for a restraining order—I wrote a story for the newspaper once about the dangers of getting a restraining order in cases of domestic abuse—I was careful to lock all of my doors when I was home.

There were moments where I felt certain that Christian and I were able to connect through my dreams, but when I would wake up disappointed after hoping to meet him in my sleep, I thought maybe I was just going crazy; perhaps the stress of the divorce and moving was too much for me.

I spent the week trying to avoid people as much as possible, because for a few days I had bruising on my arms and neck where Scott grabbed me, and I knew I couldn't possibly explain what had happened. Lizzy knocked on the door just once, and I hid in the bathroom until she left. The one time I ordered a pizza from Luigi's, the delivery kid did glance at my bruises, and I gave him a generous tip in hopes that he would just forget it. I thought I had pulled the collar of my shirt up high enough to cover the worst of the bruising, but I could see by his eyes that I hadn't done a good job. I spent most of my time alternating working on my column—knowing that if I didn't turn something in within a day or so, I would be out of a job—and daydreaming about Christian. By the end of the week, I was getting cabin fever, and planned on heading to the coffee shop again for another poetry mixer. Lizzy had left a flyer in front of my front door, held down by a pumpkin.

As I was finishing up the dishes from dinner, I realized meals were getting more meager and pathetic. I had promised myself when I left Scott that I was going to take care of myself, and my meals consisted mostly of some sort of Danish that I got from Joseph's Market in town, quickly thrown together egg and cheese sandwiches, and pizza or other quick food for dinner. That night, I promised myself that the following day I would get into town to shop or perhaps make the half-hour drive to Canandaigua's Wegmans and buy myself some proper food.

While I was wiping down the counter, my cell phone rang, and I hesitated after seeing on the caller ID that it was Nancy. Sisters had a way of knowing when something was wrong. Even when you didn't want them to know.

"Hi, Nancy," I said by way of greeting. I took the phone outside and sat on my front steps, knowing that with my poor service inside, we would have been cut off.

"Hey, little sis, how's the country?" Nancy tried out a fake country accent, sounding more like a Texan than someone living in New York City.

"It's great. You should see all the moose out here," I said, using an inside joke between the two of us to keep the conversation casual. When we were kids living in the city, I always thought that every large animal in the world was living just outside the city, hidden from the massive amounts of people surrounding New York.

"I wouldn't be surprised," Nancy said, and then brought up the one topic that I was hoping to avoid more than anything. "Not that I'd know, since you haven't invited me out to see your new place yet."

"I know, I know, I'm sorry. I've just been so busy with deadlines and trying to keep up with the house that I haven't had a chance," I told her, hoping that she would not ask for details.

"Yeah, sure, I get it. Whatever. Are you at least making some friends out there in the boonies?" Nancy always got to the heart of the matter. She also still lived in New York City, where we grew up, and truly didn't understand the draw of living upstate.

"Yes, actually, I went to a poetry reading at the local coffeehouse and I am making some friends. I'm even going back tonight," I promised.

"Poetry, huh? I thought you gave up on that 'emotional crap'? You haven't written a poem since you got married."

"That is exactly why I have started again. To resume my old life," I told my sister while absently brushing some dirt off the step.

"Well then, I am very proud of you," Nancy told me. "Speaking of your wayward ex, how is all of that going?"

I filled Nancy in on the legal details, that Scott still refused to sign any papers, and how he and I were probably going to have to go to court to fight it out.

"So, you've heard from him, then?" she asked.

"Yes, but worse, he tracked me down and showed up at my door the other night," I told her, knowing that I would omit the worst of the details.

"Oh my God, Annabelle. What happened? Why didn't you tell me sooner?" I knew that was coming.

"I didn't tell you because I didn't want you to worry, and I'm fine. He came here pleading for me to 'go home with him,' but when I told him it was over, he got mad and told me he wanted his mom's painting back." I thought that summed it up nicely.

She scoffed. "All that guy cares about is getting his way. Did you give it to him? It might make him feel the victor and leave you alone," she suggested.

"No way. If it isn't the painting, it will just be something else. Plus, I love that painting—it's the only actual gift that his mom ever gave to me," I told her.

"Yeah, well, sometimes you gotta give a little to get what you want," she advised me. I knew she was looking out for my best interest, but the statement irked me. Hadn't I given enough?

"I did not take anything from our condo except for what was implicitly mine. I have not asked him for any money for my share of what we bought together. All I want is for him to leave me alone," I quipped back, rubbing my neck. "Oh, and I want my fucking painting."

"Okay, sorry, sis. I'm just worried about you. So, what happened after you told him no?"

"He told me that I did not deserve anything. Not the painting, not the house, and certainly not to have my own happy life." I was summarizing, of course, avoiding telling Nancy about how he hurt me, and how he got chased out of the house.

"So that's it? He said you did not deserve to have your own life, and he left?" Nancy asked.

"Well, it was more dramatic than that. But I don't want to talk about it." *Like, he knocked me unconscious and tried to rape me. But the ghost who lives with me saved me, and then we made out.*

"Um-hmm. Okay." Nancy always knew when I was being elusive and also knew that there would be no breaking through the barriers anytime soon. She seemingly decided to change the subject. "So, how's the house? Do you still think it's haunted?"

I was at a loss for what to say. Would anyone ever believe me if I told them that the spirit in the house is actually a really nice and handsome guy who protects me and disappears when we kiss? I was vague once again. "Nah, I think that people are complete wusses, and that this is a very old house that makes a lot of strange noises." I could tell by the silence on the other end of the line that Nancy wasn't buying my explanation. "And if it is haunted, then the ghosts must really like me, because they don't bother me at all."

"Unless you mind someone watching you shower," she joked.

As if I hadn't thought of that. I choked out a laugh. "I'd like to think that *my* ghost is more respectful than that," I said, realizing my slip. *My* ghost.

"Okay, then," Nancy signed, letting it go. "Will you at least check in every few days, please? I don't want to read about you in the next issue of 'Haunting of Boonesville,' or whatever town you're living in. And maybe think about getting a dog. I hate to think of you all alone in the middle of nowhere."

A dog? I couldn't help but smile. With our parents gone, it really was just the two of us. "Actually, I thought about getting a dog just the other day," I told her, thinking about that creepy day in the kitchen when Lizzy first showed up.

"I am all for that!" Nancy sounded cheerful at last. "It will help keep you safe, *and* they are great ghost detectors."

That they are, indeed, I thought to myself. I had actually studied about dogs and their connection to the spiritual world after our parents died, begging Nancy to let us have a dog, hoping that it might sense them. She wouldn't go for it—and I don't blame her—as having me to care for was more than enough hard work.

I promised to check in more often, and also to invite her to stay with me as soon as the house looked decent enough for company. That appeased Nancy for the time being, and I was in good spirits once again.

I decided to grab my latest poem and head to the coffee shop early, and if Lizzy had the time, I would ask her more about her circus days. It felt good to have a friend, and a sister that was concerned for me. *So what if I had a huge crush on someone who may or may not exist,* I thought. I had been through worse. After I wrapped up the conversation with my sister, shut off the lights, and locked up, I sat in the car for a moment, looking at the house. Thoughts of a dog quickly left my mind as I thought about Christian. When I was with Christian, in my dreams, it felt so real that there was no convincing myself that it was just a dream. But then so much time passed between the dreams that I would become unsure of myself. Not only did Christian not show up in any of my recent dreams, but I was finding it harder to fall asleep and stay asleep. What I needed, I thought, while sitting in the driveway looking up at the old barn behind the house, was to be asleep for an extended period of time. I decided to stop by the Naples Apothecary on my way to the coffee shop to see what kind of all-natural sleeping pills I could find.

Chapter Eleven

"The best thing about dreams is that fleeting moment, when you are between asleep and awake, when you don't know the difference between reality and fantasy, when for just that one moment you feel with your entire soul that the dream is reality, and it really happened."

–James Arthur Baldwin

The pharmacy was just getting ready to close when I opened the doors, bells chiming above my head. I scanned the shop, small but packed with items. It was like stepping back in time. The pharmacy offered everything from five-cent candy to support hose and walkers, to last-minute gift ideas. If you want a T-shirt that said Naples, NY, in purple writing with embroidered grapes all over the front, this is your place.

As I stood in the store taking everything in and looking for where I might find some sleep aids, the woman behind the counter came out to greet me. She actually stopped sorting the paper bags of prescriptions that hadn't been picked up and walked around the counter—small-town charm at its best.

"Hello, can I help you find something?" she asked. I noticed she had a limp, and was old enough to be my grandma. Her smile was genuine, and her spectacles sat way down on her nose so that she could look at me over them. I was touched. At my old pharmacy in the city of Rochester, if they saw you coming at closing time, they would turn out the lights.

"Hi. I'm so sorry to come in right at closing. I didn't know your hours," I told her, noticing that her nametag read the name Wendy. I smiled, wondering for some reason if Peter Pan knew that she had grown up after all.

"Oh, that's okay. I don't go far. What is it that I can help you with?"

"Well, I've been having some trouble sleeping, and I was looking for some natural sleep aid."

"I'm sorry to hear that," she told me, beckoning me to follow her through the store. More Naples items, coloring books, eyeglasses. Tiny aisles packed with knickknacks and Tylenol. Wendy guided me through natural supplements such as melatonin and valerian, and asked me if it was staying asleep or getting to sleep that was the problem.

"I guess I have had a lot of my mind lately, and the harder I try to fall asleep, the harder of a time I have in getting there," I explained.

"So, something with a little more punch, I'd say. Let's see." She scanned the bottles and picked one. "This one is not under the category of 'all natural,' but it knocks me out when I can't sleep," she told me.

I laughed. "Sounds good to me. Thanks so much." I took the bottle from her and, as she was ringing me up, she asked if I was new in town. I felt like a teenager buying cigarettes, lying about my age. People buy sleeping pills all the time. It's nothing to feel secretive about. But I felt like this woman could read lines from a story on my face, in big bold letters: "I want to sleep so I can see Christian again!" Just her knowing that I was new in town made me feel like I was standing there naked.

"I am. How did you know?" I asked her.

"Well, every person in this town knows our hours, and I know most all of them by name. My name is Wendy, and I'd like to officially welcome you to our little town." Wendy shook my hand and, as I paid her, she asked me if I had met any of the other locals yet.

I had to laugh to myself, and thought, *yeah, I met a real old timer. One of the original residents, perhaps.*

"Well, I actually have been to Aunt Lizzy's coffee shop for a poetry reading, and Lizzy is just great." I didn't want to tell her that Lizzy was my neighbor, because after the reaction I got from the librarian when she found out where I lived, I wasn't ready for another bacon story.

"Ah, the coffee shop. It's where all the hippies go." Wendy rolled her spectacled eyes and laughed. "Lizzy thinks she can solve the world's problems with a cup of hot coffee and a joint. Oh, and the 'poetry,' of course." She smiled as she said it, but I felt an undercurrent of something else. No matter, I thought, small towns have their share of drama, just like the cities do. More, perhaps.

I thanked Wendy for the pills and for her kindness, and headed to the coffee shop, because hippies or not, I felt welcomed there. Just as I was reaching for the door handle, a little pamphlet stuck to the window grabbed my attention. It was a flyer for the Mountainview Animal Shelter, and the photo was of an adorable cocker spaniel, with sad eyes and a thought bubble that read, "Want to change your destiny with good Karma?" *Talk about fate*, I thought, and quickly snapped a photo of the flyer with my cell.

Aunt Lizzy's coffee shop was starting to feel very homey to me, and I had been there only twice. It was the mixture of the scents of delicious coffee mixed with almond incense, and friendly faces that seemed like old friends even after just one visit. It's a place that makes you want to curl up on one of the sofas that are in odd places throughout the shop, and meet someone new. That is odd for me, since I have always been sort of shy. When I got my job at the *Gazette*, I had to force myself to break out of my shell and talk to people. My job was to interview and get information out of perfect strangers, and sometimes it was to simply attend a community event and find a story there. I used to pretend that I was someone else when I was on an assignment. I would just imagine that I was crawling inside of myself, and I put on a face of someone who was really good at talking to strangers and liking people. It was hard at first, but became surprisingly easier as time went on. Of course, after a while, people knew me by name, and so I wasn't a stranger to them, even if they were to me.

When I left them as a full-time writer and just take assignments by freelancing, I felt like I had lost a little bit of who I was. Being the name behind the stories feels really good, and even though I am still working for the paper, it's in a much lesser capacity, and I miss being the source for community news. I couldn't stay though—I knew that in order to leave Scott, I'd have to leave the city, as well.

As I found my way to a comfy overstuffed chair at the coffee shop, I heard someone calling my name. I'm not going to lie; it was nice to have someone know me by name in a place that I had been to only twice. I knew right away that it was Ben, the guy that I met the other night. Owner of a vineyard, cute. I would have said that I don't have a type, but if I did, Ben would surely fit. If only.

Through these thoughts, I made my way over to where Ben was sitting, which was on a small sofa near the back of the room. "Hey, Ben," I said, sitting down next to him. "This place sure is busy, even at night." Looking around the room, it amazed me at how many people would want to come to a coffee shop so close to what passes for bedtime.

He smiled at me, raising his cup as if in cheer. "Lizzy's is more of a hangout than a coffee shop, I guess. Like adult day care. And it's better than a bar, I guess."

"Or a winery?" I smiled back, feeling content already.

"Trust me, after hosting wine tastings all day, the last thing I want to do is drink it." Ben smiled again, but I could sense a loneliness there. I wondered if he was married, and glanced at his ring finger. It was empty. I knew better than anyone that an empty finger did not necessarily mean that you weren't married. Besides the obvious reasons of cheating or being in construction and not wanting to take the chance of having your ring cut off you in the event of a workplace accident, plenty of people did not wear wedding bands. I actually took my own off over a year before I left Scott. I felt like the simple gold band was choking the life out of me. After a while, I couldn't stand to have it on my finger.

"Well, don't hate me for saying so, but I guess I'm kind of a wino," I confessed.

This made him laugh. "I'm more of a bourbon guy, myself. But I'll forgive you."

"Is that so?" I asked him. "So why would a bourbon guy own a winery?"

"I know," he said, shaking his head as if it didn't make sense to him, either. "It's a family business, and I took it over when my folks died. I never would have thought that I'd settle in my hometown, but here I am. I actually kind of love the place, though," he confided, "even if it is wine."

We talked for a few minutes about the usual things that people who really didn't know each other chatted about: how I liked the area, if I was able to find the only grocery store in town, what I thought of all the locals so far. Ben didn't ask me about my divorce, I didn't ask him why he didn't read his poem.

As the conversation was falling into a comfortable silence—a strange feeling to have with someone you don't really know—my phone dinged, telling me I had a text message. It was from Nancy, a cute meme of a dog waving and smiling. I showed Ben and told him that my sister thought I should get a dog.

"She doesn't think that I can handle living in the middle of nowhere by myself," I explained to him.

"Well, I think you can handle yourself just fine," he said sweetly, "but a dog is never a bad friend to have. I happen to have an in with the shelter, if you are interested."

"Oh, really?" I asked, thinking that his "in" was romantic in nature. It wasn't.

"I volunteer there two days a week," he told me. *Of course he does*, I thought. Like good looks and an awesome profession weren't enough. "When Scruffy—don't laugh at the name—died a few years back, I wasn't ready to replace him. So I decided to volunteer until I found the perfect mate again."

"Did you find one?" I asked, intrigued.

"I found dozens," he said, shaking his head. "I fell in love with every darn dog and cat in the place. So I decided I would just care for them all as much as I could, and being unable to ever choose, I go back week after week to help out with all of them."

I showed him the photo I took of the flyer, and his face lit up. "Oh I love Karma," he told me. "She is a five-year-old cocker spaniel whose owner was an elderly lady who died last year. We haven't been able to adopt her out because so many people want puppies. Little do most people realize that puppies require a lot of work, and older dogs usually come trained and happy to have a home."

"So her name is Karma?" I asked, realizing how clever the flyer was for the play on her name. Ben nodded, and right then I pretty much knew that she was mine.

"I'll put in a good word for you," he told me, and dug his business card out of his wallet. "In case you need anything, or just want to chat," he told me. As he stood up, he added, very quietly, "or if you want to have dinner with me."

Ben must have recognized the look on my face as someone who was not ready for dinner talk, and quickly added, "To help you out with Karma, of course. You'll love her. I've got to head out but seriously, you should go visit the shelter."

I watched him leave, and shook my head, again thinking, *if only*. And then, *if only what? If only I wasn't in love already*. That's when it hit me. *Holy shit, am I in love with a ghost? One that I just met?!* It was the most unreasonable thought that had ever traveled through my brain, and I've had a lot of unreasonable thoughts. Christian was dead. He was a ghost, a spirit, and one that I was not even 100 percent sure existed outside of my dreams. I felt, at that moment, like I had gone a little off my rocker. And to be honest, even if he was alive, I knew I shouldn't be falling for someone so soon after leaving Scott. I had been in rebound relationships before, but this was pushing my edges of sanity. And yet.

And yet, he saved my life. I thought about his life and his poems, the way he died for love. I thought of his eyes and his gentleness. Christian was the polar opposite of what I had been running from. He was like a magnet that I was pulled toward, even though it was crazy.

I left Lizzy's before I even got a chance to see her and say hello. Suddenly, I was in a hurry to get home and try those pills.

chapter Twelve

My bloodless heart, abandoned full of sorrow, awakens with wonder.
This feeling a forgotten mystery.
I am falling into nothingness, darkness engulfs my soul.
I am rising up to heaven, light engulfs my spirit.
This feeling I push away as I pull it back.
I know not what it is.
Love would be too much.
It cannot be.

–Christian Boyd, unrecorded poetry, after-death, 2016

Driving home that night, I thought about Ben and Christian and the very strange predicament that I found myself in. When I left Scott and moved out to Naples, I never thought that I would have a romantic notion about any man, ever again. I was actually quite happy to think of spending my days alone, with no one to be responsible for and no one telling me what to do or who to be. I liked Ben—he is cute, and he owns a vineyard (a great plus for a wine lover!)—but the person who my mind kept traveling to was not Ben. It was Christian, and I knew I had to see him again. I also knew that the only way I would be able to do that was to fall into a deep sleep.

I got there fairly easily, with just two glasses of red wine and a sleeping pill. I have always been extremely sensitive to any medication, and I figured that even though I have had a hard time sleeping, I shouldn't need more than one. Before I knew it, I was slipping in between dreams, moving from room to room in my house that was not my house, and not my lifetime. I found Christian in the kitchen, sitting at the kitchen table.

Christian looked up as I entered the room. He smiled. Although he looked exactly the same as he had in my last dream, I thought he looked better somehow. More alive, a sparkle in his eyes. "Annabelle. In ninety-nine years, no one has ever met me in their dreams on purpose."

"What is this, exactly?" I asked him. I figured out that I could talk to Christian only when I was asleep and dreaming, but I had no idea why. "Why can I see you in my dreams?"

Christian got up from the table and pulled out a chair, beckoning me to sit down. "It took me a few dozen years to figure that out myself. Then again, I had lots of time. When people sleep, their spirits are free to wander around different planes. When you dream, you are able to go back into your past as an observer, or talk to spirits that have passed on, provided they are willing and able to see you, too. Or at least, that is what I think is happening."

"Willing and able? What does that mean? I don't understand." I was confused. I noticed that the window was open, but I felt no breeze.

"All I can do is explain how I do it. I am able to enter someone's dreams, and lead them around my life. I could, say, show them a memory of mine or a glimpse into what I had seen or done in my lifetime. What I never thought possible, though, is talking to a living spirit face-to-face. That has never happened before, I suppose because there was never anybody that I wanted to talk to."

Christian sat back down, and we were facing each other across the table. I reached across the table to touch his hands, which were folded in front of him. I realized that there was no blood pumping through his body, no breath when he spoke. I was talking to a ghost, to someone who had tried to scare me, and yet I felt no fear. "So, you did give me that nightmare, the one where I saw your mother in the parlor, and you as a little boy?" I made contact with his hand, more as a test to see if I could really feel him, and when I ran my hand over his, he took my hand in his and held it. It was the sweetest gesture that I had ever experienced.

"Yes, I did that. And I am so sorry. I did not mean to frighten you. I had grown so used to scaring people away that I did not give you a chance. I am glad to have gotten to know you, but Annabelle, you can't force sleep unnaturally."

The sleeping pills. "So, you can follow me around all day, but I can't choose when I can see you? No. That's not fair. You saved me, Christian. I feel different when I am with you. Like we were meant to find each other."

He shook his head slowly, released my hands. They felt cold where we had touched. "I'm so sorry, Annabelle. There is no way that we were meant to be together. Almost one hundred years ago, I did a dishonorable thing to my soul and ended my life. I have been paying for that in time ever since, and my time here is almost up. Soon I will move on to pay the ultimate price for what I had done, but you—you have given me the greatest gift..."

I stood up quickly; the chair remaining soundless as I rose. "Wait a second. What do you mean your time here is up? What is the ultimate price? I don't understand." I was starting to feel light-headed, panicked, and I was afraid that I was about to wake up. I did not want to wake up, and I was frustrated that my time with him was so limited.

"Oh, Annabelle. Please do not be upset. If you're right, if we were meant to meet, it was perhaps for you to give me an ounce of peace, a small bit of humanity. But you cannot search for me." Christian reached out and once more grabbed my hands, beckoning me to sit again. I could not, and paced through the kitchen.

"Christian, how can you know this? It's bad enough that I have fallen in love, love, oh God." I sank down to the floor, my head in my hands. "How do you know this?" I asked him.

He spoke quietly. "It was so long ago, my death." He sat, soundlessly, on the floor next to me. He took my hand in his. "I do not know how to tell you, but I could show you. But, Annabelle, it is not a thing that I would ever wish you to witness."

"What do you mean, you can show me?" I asked him. "And yes, of course, I want to know everything that I can know about you. I want to know why we cannot be together."

He stood and held out his hand, reaching for my own. I gave it to him, and he helped me to my feet. His eyes cast a shadow of shame as he led me out of the house and to the barn. Our footsteps made no sound as we made the quick journey up a small hill, past the apple trees and the tended area of the yard. The barn looked again to be in excellent condition, not aging, sagging a bit as it was when I gaze out my back windows at it. It was very dark out, and the light of the moon lit up the barn like a stage. I turned to Christian, but he was gone, the feeling of his hand in mine already fading. I walked around to the back of the barn and peeked inside, almost yelling out as I saw Christian scribbling on a sheet of paper, tears falling from his eyes and landing on his hands as he wrote. I almost ran to him, but stopped, realizing that I must be seeing his memory. I have seen two of Christian's memories, but this one was the worst.

As I silently watched Christian climb the wooden ladder to the second floor of the barn and work a knot into a rope, I heard a rustling behind me. Goose bumps traveled the length of my spine as I turned to see a woman, looking wild and frightening in the moonlight. She was, I remembered, the woman that I had dreamed about, arguing with Christian. I watched this woman, as she watched Christian, who unceremoniously fell from the rafter, rope around his neck. Not making a move to stop him, she just stood there, under cover of the trees, glaring at him. To see her there made my skin crawl.

Lillian. I remembered her name from my dream.

I stood by helplessly as Lillian—walking right by me without hesitation—stepped out of the woods and into the barn. Heard her words as she doomed Christian to one hundred years as a ghost. The words, *it is done*, sealing the spell. It was the most powerful display of witchcraft that I had ever seen, and I understood why Christian said that his time was almost up. "A lifetime of suffering times two," I whispered in the dark barn. It made sense, considering that the average life span one hundred years ago was about fifty years. She had bound him to earth for two of her lives.

I crept through the barn, eyes avoiding Christian as his body hung lifeless from the rope. The letter that he wrote was on the dirty barn floor, and I crouched down to read it, not wanting to touch it. Not sure if I even could. It read:

My Dearest Lillian,

You can't imagine how I am feeling upon deciding to write you this letter. By the time your eyes fall on these pages, I will be gone. I cannot live without you. Your smile, your touch, the way your hair sways in the breeze; I simply refuse to go one more day without you by my side.

You have always mocked me being a poet, asked me how we would make a living when I would rather ponder the beauty and sadness of a sunrise than do the work of my father. "Man's work," you would say. I suppose the fellow I saw you with at the market must make a living with his hands, for he so expertly used them. *There I go again, as you say, I just can't let it go.*

I regret nothing more than how you left that night. I wish to blame the whisky, but it was the drink that gave me the courage to admit to you what I had seen. My dearest wish is that I could be the man you want me to be. I would raise entire barns on my own for you, plow the largest field, and harvest the most wonderful fruits, if I thought that it would win you back.

What I have realized is that you just don't love me. I have loved you since the day you were born, when I was just a boy. I knew in my heart that we would be together always.

This feeling inside me, it is frightening. I feel that my heart will stop on its own at any time, for it is racing so quickly. And yet, although I can feel my heartbeat, I feel utterly empty. I have thought of nothing but you in weeks. I cannot bear the thought of food, and my clothing hangs loose. I have nothing left to live for. Perhaps I will see my beloved parents and sister again soon. Although, it is more likely that heaven will not take me for what I have done.

Still. This torture must end tonight. Please have a wonderful life, and when you look up at night and gaze upon the stars, think of me; for it is I who will love you for eternity.

All my love,

Christian

My own tears ran down my face and fell, disappearing before they landed on the letter. I wished to wake from this dream. I stood and turned around, soundlessly screaming as I almost tripped over Christian, who was sitting on the dirty wood floor of the barn, head in his hands.

"Christian?" I softly called his name. I put my hand on his head, but it passed through him as if he were air. As if he were a ghost. "Christian?" I said again, more loudly this time. He did not look up at me. It seemed that I was still in his memory. He looked up at his body, still hanging from the rafters. He cried out, confused—seeing the impossible. Christian turned his head to a noise at the opening of the barn, and in the moon's light, a woman stepped softly inside.

Christian tried to gasp, but had no breath, and made only a jarring half yelp. "Mother?" he managed to speak the word.

The woman smiled, walking—no, gliding—over to where he sat on the floor. No dust was disturbed as she knelt down and took her son's hand. "Oh, Christian," she said to him before kissing the top of his head. "How I wish I could have stopped this."

Christian hugged her tight to him and asked, "What is happening?"

His mother closed her eyes and spoke, breaking the bad news. "It was Lillian, Christian. She was here tonight, watching you. She cast a spell on you, trapping your spirit here for the next hundred years."

Christian's mother started to weep, although her tears were not wet but sparkly; more like diamonds than tears, turning to mist as they fell. She reached out for him again and touched his face.

"Stuck here?" he asked. "As a *ghost*?" Christian stood and looked at his body. He yelled, "Haven't I suffered enough?" He spun around angrily toward his mother, but she was already fading away. She stood before him, waning in and out of vision as he tried to reach out for her.

When she spoke, it was softer and sounded like she was speaking from above. "My darling, I cannot stay with you. But I will be here when your time has come." She reached out to embrace Christian, and he held on to her, closing his eyes. When he opened them, she was gone.

"Mother? Mother!" Christian called out for her, but the only sound in the barn was of his own body, swaying gently in the breeze.

Watching this, tears soaking my shirt and face, I left the barn. Spots danced in front of my eyes, and I was dizzy. I knew I was going to faint and so I sank to the ground, letting myself fall. Moments later, when I came to, I was back in the house, still dreaming but thankfully out of Christian's memory.

Christian sat at the table with his head in his hands. Sitting at the table like that, I could still see the little boy from my dream. He looked up at me. "Annabelle, I have only a few weeks left."

I woke up sobbing, lying on top of my sheets. The sunlight was streaming through my bedroom window, birds singing right outside. I saw the rays, heard the songs of life, but could think only of loss. I had to see him again. If Lillian could cast a spell on what happened to his spirit, I reckoned I could do the same. Our time did not have to end, not yet. I reached over to my nightstand, another piece that came with the house and may have been Christian's mothers, and grabbed the bottle of sleeping pills. If one could knock me out for almost an entire night, I was pretty sure that two or three would give me more time. I vowed that the next time I went to sleep, it would be deep enough for the time I needed.

Chapter Thirteen

"I have found that when you are deeply troubled, there are things you get from the silent devoted companionship of a dog that you can get from no other source."

–Doris Day

That entire next day, I felt awful. My eyes were swollen and puffy, and I was feeling lost. Helpless. And kind of annoyed; I had come so far in my life and to feel so derailed by a man, ghost or not, frustrated the hell out of me. Not to mention how aggravating it was not to be able to finish a conversation. I decided I had to sleep longer, that I had to knock myself out well enough that I could have a strong emotion without waking myself right up.

I finally finished the first draft of my new column. It was a joke—I was giving advice on how to take care of yourself in times of crisis, yet there I was, drinking too much and taking sleeping pills so that I could see my rebound love—a ghost. It was a good thing that I had worked at the paper for so long and basically knew what my editor would want me to write about. Still, I felt bad that I was writing such crap. My advice consisted of: be sure to be kind to yourself, create a grounding practice to center your mind, let yourself feel bad but don't dwell on that feeling, and a few other pieces of guidance that I was not taking. The piece, sadly, was pure fiction. My day varied between working out and writing, which ironically is how I had imagined my time in this house to be spent.

Sending in the draft to my editor, I felt only slightly better about my work life. I knew I would freelance part time, and I did have a nest egg from my parents, but I used most of it when I bought the house and there was only enough left for me to live on for less than a year. I still needed the job.

I also needed some companionship, I thought, while wandering around my empty house. I opened my phone and clicked on the picture I took of the flyer for the shelter. It was like a lightbulb went off in my head. Nancy's comment about getting a dog, seeing the flyer, and then my conversation with Ben about the cocker spaniel named Karma. I felt bad for her, waiting for a new home after her family died. I knew what it was like to lose your family, and suddenly I knew that she belonged with me. I was such a big believer in destiny, in fate, that all signs seemed to point not just toward me getting a dog, but in my getting the cocker spaniel named Karma specifically.

Pacing around my house, I daydreamed a little about what it would have been like there if I had a dog all along. From the very first knock on the door that scared the wits out of me, I would have felt safer. It surprised me that I hadn't decided to make this leap until now. It made so much sense for me to have a dog: I love to exercise, I work from home, I'm all alone. *Well, I'm alone in the living, breathing human sense, anyway*, I reminded myself.

Since I had the day free—a great side effect of finishing my column—I decided to drive to the shelter rather than call. I knew I would need to buy dog food and about a zillion toys before the end of the day, but I was so excited that I headed right over and worry about the rest later. On the way there, I kept thinking about Christian's mother. I couldn't help but compare the way she looked in the photo I found at the library, the memory that Christian showed me, and the way she looked laid out in the parlor for her own funeral. It was surreal to witness someone's life in that way, as a living person, a dead person, and in the afterlife. I thought of her as an angel, the way her tears looked like diamond dust. It gave me such a rush of joy in that terrible moment, to know that there is an afterlife.

Those images, one after the other, consumed me until I made my way up a winding mountain road, following directions on my GPS. I arrived at what felt like the top of the world. The Mountainview Animal Shelter was absolutely gorgeous, and I quickly knew why Ben liked it here so much. A huge red barn housed the many animals, except for some horses, chickens and even a donkey grazing in the field. The barn overlooked the Naples Valley, swirls of reds and oranges glittered in the distance. You could see the outline of farms for miles, plots of land that were tilled and loved, passed on from generation to generation. I felt so grounded in that moment that the sudden barking of dogs made me jump. Someone disturbed their peace in order to greet me. I wondered if Karma was one of the barking dogs inside, and if she could sense that she was about to get a new home.

An older looking gentleman looking to be in his late sixties, early seventies, came out of the barn with a smile on his face. He had on overalls and a plaid shirt, and for a moment I felt like hugging him. There was just something about him. "Hello, miss," he said to me, extending his hand as he walked over.

I shook it, noticing how warm and soft his skin was. "Hello. It sure is beautiful here," I told him, looking around.

"That's exactly why I built this shelter here," he told me. "Nothing relaxes these poor souls like room to run and the beauty of the mountains."

I liked the way that sounded, although I was pretty sure that it was his warm personality that relaxed the animals under his charge.

I thought he had good energy, which made me smile, realizing that Lizzy was rubbing off on me.

"I can see why my friend Ben volunteers here," I said, thinking that I may just do the same. I could feel my body relax, shoulders settling back down where they should be.

"Ah, you must be Annabelle, and I am Robert. Ben told me you may be coming to adopt a dog." Robert gestured toward the barn, where the barking was coming from. It was a happy enough chatter of barks, not that crazed sound that some shelters seem to have.

I pulled out my phone and brought up the photo of Karma. "Yes, this dog specifically," I said, showing him the photo of the cocker spaniel.

Noticing right away that he frowned, I knew that I didn't want to hear what Robert was about to say. He said it anyway, of course. "I'm sorry, but Karma was adopted just this morning," he told me, and gesturing to the barn said, "but we do have many dogs looking for a home."

I know it seems childish, but I wanted to cry. And I did not want another dog. I kept imagining this dog, and it seemed so much like fate that I couldn't imagine any other outcome. I felt my shoulders sag and burning behind my eyes as I struggled to keep my composure.

Suddenly, I wanted out of there and, despite the beautiful view and charming host, I was sorry that I had talked myself into thinking that this was meant to be. "Was she adopted by a nice family?" I asked Robert, almost hoping that he would say that he didn't really like them and that they may return her.

"They certainly seemed nice," he told me, looking sorry for me. "A new husband and wife, who are just moving into the area and didn't want a puppy. It's ironic, that two people would want an older dog on the same day. Usually, the adult dogs just sit here and wait, as most folks want the little ones."

Forcing myself to smile, I thanked him and told him I'd need a few days before I looked at the other dogs. "Maybe my timing is not the best, after all," I said, putting my hand out for a goodbye shake. And then, as an afterthought, I asked him if I could leave my number with him, just in case.

"Of course you can," he told me, pulling out his own phone to put my number into. "You never know these days; I've had the most perfect dogs come back to me two or even three times. Poor souls."

Once I was in the privacy of my own car, I let myself feel the weight of disappointment. Big tears pooled in my eyes as I drove off, wondering what I did that was so bad to deserve such rotten luck.

Chapter Fourteen

"Girl, don't go away mad,
Girl, just go away."
–Mötley Crüe

A few days had passed, which I alternated between feeling sorry for myself while taking walks in the woods behind my house, and feeling sorry for myself while trying to pretend that everything was fine. I even drove to Lizzy's coffee shop but couldn't bring myself to get out of the car. I was afraid that Ben was there, and he might ask if I had been to the shelter, and I didn't want to talk about it.

One early evening, as I was watching the deer romping through my backyard, eating the apples, and seemingly enjoying the cool breeze, my cell phone range. It was about six o'clock, which I remember because my internal clock was telling me to start thinking about dinner.

The service in the house was still spotty, even though Verizon claims that my service there should be just fine, so I went into the kitchen, which seemed to get the best reception. My stomach felt heavy as soon as I saw that the number was Scott's. Hadn't I put up with enough lately, I thought. I hesitated but answered anyway, hoping that he had signed the papers. At times, it seems as if I will never learn.

"Annabelle?" the voice on the other end of the line sounded desperate. And it should have, since I had not spoken to Scott since Christian chased him off.

I gave him attitude right away, hoping to send a clear message that I didn't want to talk to him. "Seriously, Scott? You're actually calling me? I have nothing to say to you."

"Please, Annabelle. I don't know what came over me. I had been drinking and I've just missed you so much. I want you back. Please come home. You know how crazy you make me," he pleaded. Pleading would do him no good. Not only did he disgust me, but I noticed he still would never say he was sorry, and would always find a way to turn whatever happened around and blame me. It was just his way.

"That's fine, Scott. Don't take responsibility. That's not my problem anymore. Do not call me, do not come to my home, and do not call my boss. This is it—we are through." I felt strength in my voice, although my hands were shaking.

"You're making a mistake," he told me. "I don't know what's going on in that house, what kind of trap you've fallen for in there, but that house is bad news, Annabelle. You will call me to come save you."

I laughed at this, thinking of Christian running him off. "Don't hold your breath," I told him. This statement was such a cliché, I know, but it's the best I could come up with at the time. "I have to go. Goodbye, Scott." I pressed End on my phone, feeling like I did a decent job of sticking up for myself.

To the air, I said, "This sucks. Like I am the first woman to break up with her husband." Then I poured myself my first glass of wine for the night. I was thinking that after a few glasses of merlot and a few extra sleeping pills, and Christian and I could finally finish our conversation.

• • •

I knew I was dreaming right away, but it was different this time—it felt more like that first dream where I saw Christian's mother in the parlor. I walked into the kitchen, realizing for the first time that with the exception of the parlor dream, all of our encounters happened in the kitchen. I opened my mouth to call out to Christian, but fell quiet when I heard the voice of a woman. Pulse quickening, I crept around the corner, peeked into the room, and saw Christian having what looked like an emotional argument at the table.

"I'm worried about what this will mean for our country," said the woman. I strained to see her and caught glimpses of long black hair and a slight frame. She was very proper-looking, sitting straight in the high-backed chair. I found that if I stood just between the two rooms, the living room—or parlor, as it was in my dream—and the kitchen, I could stand behind the door and look through the opening. The woman was speaking matter-of-factly, but her eyes were focused on the glass that was in the hand of the man next to her. My breath caught as my eyes landed on him. Christian. Dressed exactly the same as he was when I saw him, but looking miserable. The woman continued. "Father says that our army has ninety-eight thousand men and President Wilson is calling for more."

When Christian spoke to the woman, his speech was slurred. "Darling Lillian," he said, smiling sweetly. "Why do you care? You know that women needn't be concerned with anything so serious."

Lillian. My heart rate picked up again, and I felt the pull of jealousy mixed with anger for being privy to this conversation.

Lillian looked up slowly, her face dangerous with anger. "Christian," she purred with a sweet smile, while looking through the slits of her eyes. "We have talked about this. I have dreams. I want to make a difference."

"Yes, of course, but Lillian," Christian said, and paused to grasp her hand, making me want to cry out as jealousy coursed through my blood. He squeezed her hand, and she cringed in response. "I was not aware that you were to make a difference by giving your body to all of Ontario County."

I did not want to see any more, but I did not know how to get out of this dream. *It figures*, I thought. *This is the one time that I actually want to wake up and cannot.*

At his words, the truth seemed to dawn on her one beautiful feature at a time. "Christian, you have it all wrong." She struggled out of his grasp, but immediately took his hands back in hers. "I... well, I..."

Christian threw her hands off him and got up so quickly that he knocked his chair over. "What kind of fool do you take me for? I *saw* you, when I went to town to Mr. Wilson's meat shop. He was out and as I walked past the blacksmith, I saw you there with that Greer boy, and don't tell me you were shopping for a shield!"

Christian was so close to her face, and Lillian did not move. Nor did she back down. Instead, she laughed at him. "A shield? Oh please, Christian, a dumb girl like me? I just like to watch the metal get hot and harden." Lillian got up and walked toward the door, yanking it open. She stood in the doorway a moment, looking out toward the fields. She lifted her hand and tucked her hair behind her ear, shoulders softening, as if the anger were draining from her body. "I'm not like most women, Christian. I cannot be the wife you need me to be." Lillian spoke softly as she wiped a tear as it fell down her cheekbone. "I cannot stay home while you earn our living. And honestly, darling, you spend so much time with your paper and pen, whatever time you aren't working is not really spent with me, anyway." Lillian stepped through the doorway.

"Where are you going?" he asked her, as he sat back down and put his head in his hands.

"Where am I going, darling? I'm moving on. I have to." And with that, she shut the door quietly behind her, and was gone.

Sinking to the floor right where I had been watching them, I closed my eyes. I felt like a fool. Why would Christian show me this? As if beckoned by my thoughts, I felt him sink to the floor in front of me. I opened my eyes, wiping a tear of my own, and found that his eyes were shimmering as well.

"Why, Christian? Why would you show me that? Why would you show me her?"

"Because you are acting recklessly, Annabelle," he told me, and he took my hand in his. "You have said that you love me, but you don't know all of me. Lillian left me because I was not masculine enough for her—because I loved poetry and the written word."

He looked ashamed, which made me feel sorry for him. "There is nothing wrong with being different, Christian. I am a writer. I would have respected that in you."

He cut me off. "You don't understand. I did not want to join the fighting, in the war. I wanted to stay home with my family, and Lillian. It was soon after my death that the military drafted men to fight, and I would have been made to go. She saw me as a coward. And worse, when I saw that she had been with another man, I was furious with her. I lost my temper, made worse by the drink. I am not perfect, don't you see? I am not worth what you are risking."

"Well, I don't see it that way," I told him, struggling to find the words to make him see himself how I did. "I see a man who had his heart broken. You did not see the world the way other people around you saw it, and that makes you special, not a coward. And as for you losing your temper, it's not like you berated her or hit her. You had a right to be angry."

Christian smiled slightly, but still shook his head in disagreement. "I frightened her," he said.

"She was a witch who sentenced you to a miserable existence. I can't imagine that she was too frightened," I told him. I felt sad for him. Seeing how miserable he had been, and the memory of his suicide, broke my heart. "I am so sorry for what happened to you."

"It's okay, Annabelle. I don't need for you to be sorry, I just needed for you to see." He leaned in and brought his lips to mine, and I kissed him back. He opened his eyes and met my own, and when I leaned in again, he did not pull away. Ghost or not, for that kiss, he felt as solid as any man I've ever kissed.

When I woke up the next morning, I felt giddy even through my wine-and-sleeping-pill-induced hangover. I lay in bed, thinking about our kiss, when I realized I did not get any answers that I was looking for. I did not get the chance to tell him I could stop him from leaving me. Christian still thought his time was up. I was still in love—more in love, actually—with a ghost. Our time together was limited, and I couldn't even talk to him about it. I wanted to find that deep sleep again, to see him, but I now knew that he could surprise me with another memory and avoid my questions. Pacing my bedroom, I absently scanned my bookcase over and over again as I walked back and forth, matting the carpet down with my bare feet. My eye kept stopping on the *Encyclopedia of Magical Herbs* by Scott Cunningham, one of the few Wiccan books I kept when I moved in with Scott. He hated magic and energy healing and anything that seemed too "hippie," and so I gave it all up for him.

My pacing slowed as I was thinking of magic, spirits, and that plane in between the living and the spirit world. Magic connects all things. That's it, I realized. I would use an incantation to invoke Christian. He was so powerful the last time I used magic, and that was a simple meditation. This time, I would summon the Goddess Aphrodite herself if I had to.

Chapter Fifteen

"That old black magic has me in its spell, That old black magic that you weave so well; Icy fingers up and down my spine, The same old witchcraft when your eyes meet mine."
–Johnny Mercer

Kismet. That autumn night, I felt it everywhere. Finding this house, my spiritual history, not being run off by Christian during those first weeks. Fate. Meeting Lizzy, the coffeehouse and poetry readings, giving me a greater connection to Christian, a poet himself. Destiny. A full moon on the night I have chosen to connect to Christian. I had not tracked the moon in some time, yet that night it was full and bright, sending light into the kitchen, illuminating my altar. I never stopped to think of what could go wrong. I had not cast a spell in years, and even then, they were beginner spells. They made me feel strong and powerful, but there was no danger in doing them.

Before I began, I took a cleansing bath, to purify both my energy and my intentions. I slowly dressed in simple black leggings and a long black tunic. At the stroke of midnight, I opened my circle, using a crystal necklace to direct an imaginary circle of energy around me, starting in the east and working in a clockwise motion. I placed a candle at the eastern tip, a beacon to guide Christian to me. The candle I chose was purple, associated with psychic matters and to assist in connection with the unseen realms. I sat in the circle, eyes closed, breathing in for a count of three, and letting my breath out for that same count. Three breaths, to represent mind, body, and spirit. To ground me. My hands lay open, resting on my knees. On my altar lay a sprig of lavender and a glass of wine, my offerings to the Goddess of Love, which I intended to bury under the apple tree under the light of this very moon when I finished and closed my circle.

Before I spoke, I could feel the energies shifting around me. The old feeling came back to me, not of power exactly, but of feeling strong, like I am a part of something much, much larger than myself. I spoke:

Christian Boyd, I summon thee.
Leave your darkness and enter my light.
From death to life come back to me,
Be with me here on this night.

I felt a slight breeze in the room; the air moving past my body not only faster but colder. The house was still silent, though, no hint of Christian's whisper.

Again I spoke, louder this time.

Christian Boyd, I summon thee.
Leave your darkness and enter my light.
From death to life come back to me,
Be with me here on this night.

That is when I felt him, behind me, his breathless body taking form. I had done it. I opened my eyes and uncrossed my legs, going up on my knees to turn around. Smiling, I reached out for him and let out a happy hoot of success. That happy sound died from my lips as I saw Christian, gasping for air, the frayed noose around his neck, hanging in the kitchen. His eyes bulged and his legs kicked madly. I looked for a way to get him down, but the rope was not attached to anything; he was just hanging there, suspended by air, slowly dying—again—right in front of me. The blood must have been pooling in his body from lack of oxygen, because I could see it right through his skin, spots of purple and blue. The rope around his neck seemed to tighten by every half second.

"Oh my God. Oh my God. What the fuck? Christian!" There was an impenetrable energy field around his body. I could not touch him, could not help him. A wind was kicking up in the kitchen, my hair blowing into my mouth, into my eyes. I was killing him all over again, making him suffer as he did almost one hundred years ago.

I dove into the circle that I had created, knocking over the candle and the wine in one motion. Wax stuck to my hand as I broke the circle, retracing it counterclockwise, unable to speak.

As quickly as Christian had appeared, he vanished. Taking baby steps over to the space where he had hung, I lifted my hands and felt the air. It felt empty.

"Oh, Goddess. What have I done?" I asked the air around me. "I am so, so sorry." When I summoned Christian, I summoned him at the moment of his death. I called him back from the shadows without thinking it through.

My tears throughout the night would not stop falling. I took a shower to try to clear my energy, sobbing my way through a sopping wet mess of toilet paper. My heart hurt, pumping blood into a body that no longer wanted to live. Barely drying off, I sank down on my bed, not having the will to even put any clothes on. The bottle of sleeping pills sat on the bedside table, along with a half-bottle of merlot. I took a handful of pills, just to sleep. It was all I wanted, to sleep and forget that I had basically murdered the man I love. I knew that didn't make sense, but it was all I could think of, as I swallowed the last of the bottle and closed my eyes. *I am a murderer. I am a murderer.*

As I was drifting away, pulled under by the wine in my system mixing with the pills, I realized I was clutching the sprig of lavender, my lifeline to the other realm, to my love. I ran my fingers over the herb and all I could think of was the fray of the rope around Christian's neck. Distantly, I heard my phone ringing, the tiny chirping of my ringtone fading until sleep pulled me under.

Chapter Sixteen

"Heart beats fast
Colors and promises
How to be brave
How can I love when I'm afraid to fall
But watching you stand alone
All of my doubt, suddenly goes away somehow
One step closer"
–Christina Perri, *A Thousand Years*

Although I wished with all my might that I was dead, I knew that I was dreaming. I had the lavender in my hand, and I was standing under an apple tree under the full moon. I guessed that my thoughts brought me here, to where I thought I should bury my offering. Looking around helplessly, seeing well enough in the light of the moon, but not knowing what I was supposed to do. I looked toward the back of the property, where the old barn stood. In my reality, it was falling down and really should be restored, but in my dream, it was a beautiful structure. As if the moon were shining a spotlight through a loft opening, I could see into the barn, and my eyes rested immediately on a wooden beam that ran from one end of the barn to the other. I could picture the length of the wood, the way it splintered slightly when feet shuffled slowly across it, rope dangling between them. Christian's beam.

As if the very thought of him had brought him to me, Christian was suddenly standing right beside me, looking up at the barn, too. He was there so quickly that I let out a scream, which seemed to snap him out of his reverie.

"Annabelle," he said, and embraced me, wrapping his arms around my waist and pulling me to him. I quickly backed away and held him at arm's length, looking over his face, confused.

"Christian, are you okay? I am so sorry." Tears flowed down my cheeks, sparkling in the moonlight as he wiped them away.

"I'm okay," he told me. "I wasn't. I felt like I was alive again at last, but the very second I felt alive, like I was breathing in air again, the rope was around my neck and I was hanging there, in the kitchen. But then it was over, and I was right back in the house, as usual, and you were gone. After a while, I saw you standing out here."

Christian held on to me and did not let go, but I stepped back. "Do you mean that you did not bring me here, in my sleep?"

"You, Annabelle, are amazing me more each day," he told me, as he again reached out to touch my hand. I let him hold it this time, feeling a warmth run through our intertwined fingers. "You brought me here, it seems."

"But I could have killed you." Even as I said those words, I knew they were wrong. Christian was already dead.

"No. Not killed me. But you did have to witness my awful demise." Christian brought a hand to his neck, absently stroking the mark.

Looking at him in the moonlight, blue eyes scanning my face, there was not a single thing in the world that seemed more important than just being there, with him. He seemed so solid, so real that, while I questioned my sanity, I knew that there was one thing I wanted more than anything. More than any question answered, more than the apology that was forming on my lips. I wanted to feel him close to me, and I did not want to let go.

I stepped close to him, putting his hands around my waist, and very slowly I kissed his neck. I felt, more than heard, a moan escape his lips. Did I feel his breath catch? No. But I did feel him tighten his arms around me. My pulse quickened. His pulse, of course, remained absent, but nonetheless, he let me lead him across the lawn and into the kitchen. I tried to walk, hand in hand with him, into my room, but he shook his head and led me upstairs to his own bedroom.

I was disoriented for a moment. When I dreamed with Christian, I never knew which version of the house I would be seeing. This time, we were in his house, as it was when he was alive. He sat down on the tiny bed, ducking his head to not hit it on the slanted ceiling. I did the same, but instead of sitting down next to him, I straddled his long legs and gently pushed him back on the bed. Feeling the feminine power within me, knowing that I had orchestrated this union, and still cursing my magic, but feeling the rush of it all the same, I took off my shirt and unclasped my bra. Dream or not, this was completely real.

I felt drawn to Christian, as I had never felt drawn to any man. When he touched my breast, it felt like he was reaching into my soul. In a way, I believe he was.

I kissed him, taking my time, slowly. He felt solid, not like a ghost at all, but like any other living man. I wondered where in his time he brought me. Is this his room, while he was still alive, or just after his death? I wondered many things, but acted only on one. I leaned down and kissed him. Felt his body respond to me as I did so. He pulled me down to him and nibbled on my earlobe, my neck, my mouth. He playfully bit at my neck, the tiny bit of pain giving me the wonderful sensation of knowing he was real. Christian looked me in the eyes as he fumbled with the snap on my jeans, and I knew in that moment that I would do anything to be with him.

Finally, both of us completely naked, I leaned down and kissed him, and never closed my eyes, even for a moment, as we made love. I was afraid that if I closed them, I would awaken in my own bed, in my own time, alone.

As soon as he entered me, I felt an explosion of light and energy coursing through my body. Colors everywhere—pinks and violets and shades of color that I had never imagined—surrounded my body, touched the walls, traveled through my eyes and down my arms. I breathed in and tasted something sweet, like the sugar cubes my grandma used to keep in a jar in her cupboard, melted on my tongue. When I climaxed, I felt all of the light whoosh through me at once. I looked down and saw that I was glowing, actually glowing like a star on a clear night. At that moment, I understood what I had learned through my study of energy about the universe and how we are all connected. At that moment, I thought I understood everything, and I was afraid of nothing.

As we lay together after, my hand running up and down the length of his spine and him stroking my hair, I felt like we had found a way to be together, and that everything would be just fine.

So tired, I finally closed my eyes and whispered, "I love you."

Christian put his lips on my forehead, let them rest there for a moment before answering. I was already half-asleep when I heard his reply. "I love you. Goodbye, sweet Annabelle."

Chapter Seventeen

*"Never say goodbye because goodbye means going away
and going away means forgetting."*
–J.M. Barrie, ***Peter Pan***

Goodbye?

My eyes opened. I was in my own bed. Nine a.m. I never slept that late. Looking around, I saw all my things—books on the shelf, brush on the dresser, wineglass on the nightstand—and ran to the bathroom to verify that it was my bathroom and not an old closet. I was in my time, and I was alone. Did goodbye mean for the night, or forever? I wondered if we had really made love, or if I just dreamt the whole thing. Looking into the mirror, I saw a tiny mark on my neck. Leaning over the sink to get a closer look, I realized the mark was a nibble, from Christian.

I stroked my fingers over the mark. It was something, at least. Something real.

Just then my stomach rolled, and I saw spots in my vision, the feeling like I was going down at any moment. My head spun, like it did when I was in high school, and tried to keep up with my sister and her friends during drinking games. With no chance of stopping it, I threw up, just making it to the toilet in time. I can almost always breathe myself through nausea. This was different. I felt like I had been drugged. The pills. Just then, I remembered I had taken the rest of the bottle. I was sick again, emptying the contents of my stomach into the bowl. I rested my head on the side of the porcelain tub and thought about everything that had happened the night before. The incantation to bring Christian to me. The horrible way in which he appeared, straight out of the moment of his death. And after, the moonlight. Christian. His bed. I was confused and hungover, and scared about what I had done.

Sleep seemed like the best option, and I slowly shuffled from the bathroom into the bedroom, not bothering to get under the covers. I remember wanting to take some Advil for my headache, but didn't think that was the best idea for my body.

I slept, dreamless, until after noon. When I woke up, I felt better—kind of a miracle, I think. But that's when my brain took over and started obsessing over Christian. Everything that I had thought I understood the night before seemed confusing and unanswered all over again. I wandered around the house for a while, feeling lost. I put some ground coffee into the electric percolator, filled it with water, plugged it in, and got two coffee cups out of the cupboard. While it was brewing, I went upstairs to Christian's room. On my way up the narrow steps, I somehow thought that I would see his room as I had the night before, but when I reached the top step and saw only empty beds and boxes, I realized how dumb that thought was.

To the empty room I told myself, "This isn't your first rodeo, Annabelle. Of course the room is empty." This isn't my first rodeo. That's what my dad used to say when he left for work and my mom told him to be careful. He would pull her toward him and kiss her, saying, *"This isn't my first rodeo, darlin'."* He knew what he was doing, and I guess so did I. Somehow, I was becoming an expert on dating a ghost. The thought made me laugh, the sound bouncing off the walls of the empty room. Saying that phrase aloud made me think about my parents. After they died, I tried to feel a connection with their spirits. I would talk to them and wait for an answer, believing that if I concentrated hard enough on the silence, I would hear their voices. It never happened, and finally I stopped believing in the afterlife altogether.

Thinking back on those days made me feel a little giddy, knowing that my parents must have been there all along, just out of my reach. I laughed again, feeling like maybe I was cracking up a bit, and yet I knew I wanted to see Christian again. I kept thinking about the goodbye. What did that mean? Goodbye forever, or goodbye for the night?

I crossed the barren room and sat on the bed nearest the wall where we had spent the night. It was just a bedframe with an old box spring and mattress, and I wondered if it was the same one that Christian had slept in. I doubted it, but then again, who knows? The chair was gone, and I wondered where it had ended up.

Closing my eyes, I tried to feel if Christian's spirit was in the room. I needed to know what he meant when he said goodbye. I put my hands on my knees, palms up, and tried to go inward. Breathed slowly, purposefully. Imagined the air filling my lungs, swirling around the inside of my body, making space between my cells. Let it out slowly, pushing my life force into the room.

I thought I heard a noise. "Christian?" I called into the empty room.

Nothing. I looked around the room, and was dismayed to have felt nothing. No sign of Christian's spirit there with me. I put my hand to the mark on my neck again, my one tangible connection to him, and as I did, there was a knock on the kitchen door. For the umpteenth time since moving into the house, I jumped up with a yelp, feeling the familiar feeling of pins and needles traveling through my body while my heart jumped around my chest. Even when you are in love with the ghost haunting your house, you still tend to be jumpy.

I wondered how my life would be different if Karma had been at the shelter. Not only would I have a friend, but I'd have someone else with me to hear the noises, maybe even give me a warning that someone was at the door before they scared me to death. It had occurred to me that I could get a different dog. Puppies were always a good option, as they stir up all the old energy in the house with their playful banter, and I was sure that there were plenty of dogs of all ages to choose from. The only problem was that every time I thought of having a furry friend at my side, I pictured that little cocker spaniel. Once I convince myself that something is meant to be, I have a hard time letting go.

I went back down the stairs and was happy to look out through the door in the kitchen to see Lizzy standing there, my one and only true friend in the world, dressed in paint-stained overalls and a colorful knit hat. I opened the door for her as she stepped inside. Bright red leaves swirled in with her feet, coming to rest on the kitchen floor.

Lizzy seemed to bring happiness with her wherever she went. I shut the door tightly behind her, hoping to keep the chill of the fall air from following her inside, and couldn't help but smile at her outfit. "You look, ah, really cute," I told her.

Lizzy looked down at her overalls and gave me a little curtsy. "My motto is, if you're not comfortable in your clothes, you're not comfortable in your life." She put her hands on her hips and nodded her head in affirmation.

"I couldn't agree more," I told her. "And what brings you by on this chilly day?" I asked.

"Oh, you know, I was just checking on you. I tried to call you last night but your phone went to voice mail. No use pulling any punches—you're one eccentric woman, and I happen to like you very much. Something tells me that you could use some company from time to time."

"I'm eccentric?" It was all I could think to say, as no one had ever called me that before. Here stood before me a lady wearing paint-stained overalls and a hat with a dozen different colors in absolutely no pattern, and she was calling me eccentric. I was... amused.

"Yes, honey, you are." Lizzy took off her hat, picking a leaf off one side. "First, you move into this big old house all by yourself, asking questions about it in the Naples Library—oh don't look at me like that, this is a small town and just about everyone comes through my coffee shop. You visit the shop and start to make friends, get to know the locals. Then you disappear for two weeks, not even answering the door when I knocked, and yes, I know you were home. Now you are out and about again, and last night there was a rainbow of color coming from a room upstairs. So, either you are having a rager and not inviting the neighbors, or you, my dear, are eccentric."

I was speechless. She saw those colors?

Lizzy went right on, barely breathing through her speech. "I know I'm rambling, and I hate to be nosy, but I just wanted to check on you. That's all." She smiled at me, took a deep breath. "Is that fresh coffee I smell?"

"Oh, Lizzy, I'm sorry," I told her, having forgotten my manners completely. "Would you like a cup? I just brewed it."

"Would a coffee shop owner like a cup of coffee? Does a beaver pee in the stream?"

I opened the cabinet to grab a second mug when I realized that there were already two sitting on the counter. I shut the cabinet and glanced at Lizzy to see if she saw that, too.

"Oh, are you expecting someone?" she asked me.

"Just you, I guess," I told her, laughing at myself. "I must have a sixth sense after all," I said, and poured two cups. "Milk? Sugar?"

Lizzy put her pointer finger over her lips, as if she were about to tell me a secret. "Don't tell anyone, but I take mine with a cube of sugar."

A cube of sugar. That sweet taste when I was with Christian. The colors. I was so confused and wanted to talk about it.

I set the two cups down, Lizzy's with one scoop of sugar and mine with a splash of almond milk. I sat down across the table from Lizzy and fiddled with my cup.

"You look like you're at a confessional," Lizzy told me before picking up her coffee and taking a sip.

"Lizzy, I'm not eccentric. I'm pretty low key. Things have been pretty crazy around here, and, well, I feel like I'm losing my mind." Just saying that to her made me feel better. Like I was not all alone.

Lizzy took a careful sip of her coffee, looking intrigued. "You know what they say about coffee shop owners. We are basically therapists. Just one step below a bartender!" Lizzy laughed and then patted my hand with her own. "Really, though, honey, what's going on?"

I decided to risk it. To risk my new neighbor and friend thinking I'm completely nuts, to risk someone telling me that what I am saying must be a mistake, to risk upsetting Christian by telling our secret. I had to tell someone. I could feel Christian's absence, like how a baby fawn knows when her mother has died.

"Okay, I'm going to tell you. You are going to think I'm nuts and you will probably run from here before I am even finished." I took a deep breath. It reminded me of the last time I dumped the contents of my soul on Lizzy, and she didn't shun me then. "I am in love with Christian," I told her.

Her eyebrows shot up. "Christian, as in the ghost who is haunting your house, Christian?" she asked me. "How on earth do you explain that one?" Lizzy had her elbows on the table and propped her chin on her folded hands, as if waiting for me to spin a tale that she couldn't believe.

I rolled my eyes at her. "Oh, don't look at me like that," I quipped. "I haven't forgotten about your circus days!"

Lizzy cocked her head and gave me a "bring it" motion with her hands, and when she smiled, I noticed it reached her eyes easily.

I wasn't sure how to explain. "Do you believe in magic?" I asked her.

Lizzy smiled, nodding once. "Oh, honey, now you're talking my language," she said, giving me the courage to go on.

I talked for an hour, until our coffees went cold and my stomach grumbled. I told Lizzy everything, about how I first met Christian, about how we found a way to connect in my dreams, how I learned so much about his past with Lillian (that awful woman) and how he died and was cursed to remain here for one hundred years. And worse, how that time was almost up. I even told her about my conversations with Ben. I felt like I was in a weird love triangle while I was talking, yet I was losing the one who captured my heart. I felt hopeless, and tired, and yes, a bit crazy. The only part I did not tell her was how I brought Christian to me, hanging and dying. It was too personal, too intimate. Plus, I figured she would think I was absolutely nuts. And truthfully, I was ashamed and embarrassed about causing him that pain all over again.

When I got to the part about being with Christian the previous night, I showed Lizzy the tiny mark on my neck, already fading but still visible, and she gasped. "Are you sure it's not a scratch mark? Food allergy?" She touched my neck.

"I'm sure. Not a scratch."

"Maybe a bug got you in your sleep. You know, fall here can dredge up the most awful insects, and..."

I stopped her. "Lizzy, I'm sure. You saw the crazy light show last night, and I assure you I do not have a laser show set up in my guest room."

"Okay. So, let's suppose for a minute that you are in love with Christian, who is a ghost. What's that going to be like for you? You can't exactly go out for dinner or invite friends over."

I laughed, wondering if Christian was listening to any of this. "I know. I know, but I have bigger fish to fry when it comes to Christian. I'm not sure how much longer he's going to be around." It hurt me to even say that.

Lizzy looked about as perplexed as I felt about the whole situation. "What do you mean, honey? He's dead. Where is he going?"

I told her about watching him hang himself, and how Lillian cast the spell, and the strange goodbye that I got before waking up. "The worst part is, I can't even have a normal conversation with him because he doesn't stick around long enough."

Lizzy drained her cup, unconcerned with the fact that she just drank cold coffee. Her gaze was distant, and she seemed to wrestle with a thought. "I still don't know how I feel about all of this—and I do think that maybe you bumped your head and dreamed the whole thing—but I do have a friend who is a medium. You could have her over, and, ah, communicate with Christian. Kind of like couples' therapy for the supernatural?"

All I could picture was the lady from *Poltergeist*; the one who brought Carol Anne back, screaming "Come into the light, Carol Anne!" I laughed. "A medium? Don't they just piss off spirits generally?" Not that I didn't believe that a medium could make the connection that I sought. My hesitation was partly because there are many people out there claiming to "make contact" but do nothing but take advantage of a grieving loved one, and partly because it was frustrating for me to think that a true medium could just sit down and talk to Christian, while I had to practically comatose myself just to see him.

"Only if they don't want to be bothered. And it seems that Christian likes your company," Lizzy said, waggling her eyebrows up and down while looking at the mark on my neck.

I sighed, feeling like I was running out of options. "Alright," I told her. "What's the worst that can happen?" Right at that moment, the lights dimmed, and the radio played that old-fashioned music. Lizzy's eyes looked like giant saucers, and she grabbed my hand over the table. "It's okay, Lizzy. He's just playing our song."

Chapter Eighteen

"Allow the power to flow through you. Don't try to capture it. You wish only to borrow it."
—**G.G. Collins**, *Reluctant Medium*

It had been three days since Lizzy and I sat in the kitchen and talked. I had not seen Christian since the night before that, when we made love. Waiting for Lizzy to get back to me about her medium friend, I stalked my phone, checking it every half hour at least. I had ignored every other text or call that I had gotten, including a call and a text from Nancy, a voice mail from Scott telling me he would sign the papers if we could just get together for coffee or lunch—not happening—and a text from my editor telling me that the revisions to my column was already three days overdue and what on earth am I doing out in Bumfuckville if I'm not writing?

I didn't answer any of them.

I was a woman obsessed, only thinking of Christian: Was he still a spirit? Did I miss my opportunity to be with him? Did he love me? Was he just silently watching me? I wondered about that a lot. Every time I took my clothes off to get in the shower or change, I wondered if he was silently watching me. Finally, on a foggy evening that looked like the scene was plucked right out of *The Amityville Horror*, as I sat on my front stoop and wished for the thousandth time that Christian would show me a sign that he was still around, my phone vibrated in my hand. A text from Lizzy, telling me that her friend Melissa would be able to meet with me at the house the very next night, and would I like Lizzy to join them?

I thought about that for a while. I didn't really want anyone else involved with my relationship with Christian, and I had reservations about letting a medium into the house, mostly worried that it would piss Christian off. I thought about the way he actually threw Scott out of the house. I was desperate, though, and actually found comfort in the thought of Lizzy being there.

I texted her back:

Yes plz, I would love that. What time?
Eight p.m.?
Perfect. What should I do to prepare?

Her reply took a few minutes to come through. The little text bubble on my phone got bigger in my mind the more I stared at it.

Melissa says all you need is an open mind. But no booze, it interferes with the energy.

Oh, great. Melissa the Medium has rules. Every time I saw Christian in my dreams, he has given me wine. But whatever, it was one night, and it's not like we were having a sleepover.

I texted her back, trying to seem positive about the whole thing.

Okay, makes sense. See you tomorrow. Thx so much!

· · ·

After another dreamless night, I woke up frustrated and ready for someone to give me some clue as to what was going on. I was feeling a mixture of love, loneliness, and to be honest, anger. I didn't see Christian as a love 'em and leave 'em type of guy, but that's pretty much what he did with me. Was I just an amusing side note for him, a way to spend his time before he could finally move on and find Lillian in the afterlife? And what did that say of me? I've been in rebound relationships before, but with a ghost? No. This had to be something more, and I was about to find out. Or so I hoped.

I spent the day pacing the house; cleaning and walking in circles. I tried a few times to work and revise my column, but I just couldn't concentrate. I cleaned the upstairs bathroom, the downstairs bathroom, the kitchen, living room—parlor?— bedroom, and upstairs bedroom that I was using as my office. I went into the room that was Christian's, but I could not make myself clean in there; the room felt like a shrine to him, one that I did not want to disturb with Mrs. Meyers cleaner and my vacuum. Instead, I cleaned the rest of the house like it was my life's mission.

As last, the clock in the kitchen struck eight, and I was ready.

• • •

Melissa was not at all like I expected her to be. I was picturing someone like Zelda Rubinstein, who was the eccentric medium in *Poltergeist*. She is definitely eccentric, but instead of small and with a whispery voice, Melissa was tall and thin, and had a commanding, booming voice. If I were a spirit and this particular medium told me to speak, I would speak. She and Lizzy showed up together, having walked over from Lizzy's house. I could only imagine what Lizzy told her already and what she thought of me.

After the introductions from Lizzy, I showed them inside the kitchen and lit the candles at the table. Melissa helped herself to a glass of water, looking around the room and dimming the light. "So, you are a Wiccan?" she asked me, glancing over her shoulder casually in my direction.

"Oh no, not really," I told her, wondering just how much about me Lizzy had shared. "I used to be, when I was younger, but kind of grew out of it when I got married."

Melissa smiled, and walking toward me said, "You are what you are in your heart, so you may say that you used to be, or that you just dabble here and there, but you can't dim that light forever. You have a great respect for nature and for the cycle of life in here." She stood in front of me and touched right above my heart and then put her hand lightly on my head. Lizzy had been quiet since we walked into the kitchen, but I could see her watching us from the corner of my eye. "But you have to learn it in here. If what Lizzy says is true, you may have to let go. Let's begin."

I was too stunned to say anything, yet I felt a tear escape my eye and run down my cheek. We sat at the kitchen table in a circle. We must have looked like quite the crew; Lizzy in a pair of strawberry-embroidered overalls, looking like a cross between a hippie and a farmer, Melissa sitting ramrod straight, her black hair flowing halfway down her back, her piercing greenish eyes shut for the moment. And myself, feeling as nervous as a schoolgirl on the first day of a new school—anxious and hopeful, but waiting for something to go wrong. Lizzy sensed my feelings and leaned over and grabbed my hand, the kind gesture making those tears escape again.

It was almost fully dark outside as Melissa, eyes closed but fully aware of the room, asked for Christian to join us. Her voice was powerful but kind as she said, "I would like to thank the energies in this house for allowing us to be here. Thank you to our spirit guides. Christian Boyd, if you are with us, please let us know. You are safe with us."

We waited in silence for several minutes before Melissa spoke again. "Christian," she said more softly, "I feel your presence, come out from the shadows."

I instantly thought of how I summoned Christian from his death, hanging from a noose, gasping for air. Putting my head down, I hoped Melissa could not read my thoughts or see my shame.

Suddenly a gentle gust of air came through the room, blowing out the candles, leaving darkness where there was light. The smell of wick filled my nose.

"Christian Boyd, is that you?" Melissa asked, eyes still closed. I wondered how she had the courage to close her eyes against the darkness like that. She smiled and nodded her head, hands open on her lap as if receiving light.

My eyes were on Melissa, and out of the corner of my vision I could see that Lizzy's were, as well. I expected Melissa's voice to change and become Christian's. I expected her head to roll back and her eyes to stare vacantly. I expected something drastic or frightening. Instead, when she spoke, it was her own voice, filled with kindness. "It is nice to meet you as well, Christian," she said to what seemed like the entire room.

I looked all around for him but saw nothing. I thought I could feel his presence, but I also wanted to feel his presence so badly that I wasn't sure what I felt. Was he really here? I couldn't help but wonder why he would show himself to a stranger, but not to me.

"Annabelle?" It was Melissa, startling me from my whirlwind of thought. "You can't see Christian because he is a spirit, and you are not asleep. Your conscious mind filters things like spirits to protect you. You can see him in your dreams because it feels safer for your mind that way." It was like she plucked the question right from my mind. She continued, "I can see him in my mind, and hear him, but not through my ears. But he is here with us. He is all around you."

Not sure if I should laugh or cry, I whispered, "Can you tell him I love him, please?"

"He knows," Melissa told me. "It's very complicated for him, to feel that emotion after all these years."

I tried to interject, but Melissa held her hand up, telling me to wait. "Just let me listen, Annabelle."

So, we sat there, in silence, for what seemed like an eternity. The night got even darker, and I swear the owls and frogs and anything else chirping or making noise out in the woods were creeping even closer to the house. Melissa just sat there, looking as if she were merely meditating at my kitchen table. Finally, she spoke. "I understand, but please, be careful with her," was all she said before opening her eyes and chugging an entire glass of water.

I couldn't stop myself, asking, "Well?" before she could even put the glass down. My hands were shaking, as my mind was telling me over and over again that Christian did not love me back.

Melissa took a deep breath and picked up the matches, lighting each of the three candles on the table. "I like the ambiance," she told us, shrugging. Once she was finished, she looked at me and shook her head sadly. "He loves you, Annabelle, he does. But as you already knew, his time on our plane of existence is almost up, and he does not even know his fate. He doesn't want to hurt you any more than he already has." She stopped talking when she noticed that I had more tears running down my cheeks.

"But he's only hurting me by leaving me before he has to," I pleaded with her. "I understand, I get it, but I want to be with him until I can't. I already love him; he can't take that back."

Melissa sat up tall and shook her hair from her face. "And that is why he is going to meet you tonight, when you go to sleep. He told me about the pills, Annabelle, and he doesn't want you to put yourself at risk for him."

I couldn't help but roll my eyes. After everything that we had seen and done together, he should know that nothing could stop me. "I know. I will try," I told her.

"And Annabelle, Christian wants you to be happy. That means moving on once he is gone," Melissa told me softly.

I nodded my head and got up to get a tissue, noticing that Lizzy had been sitting in silence pretty much since they got to the house. "Lizzy? Are you alright?" I asked her.

She rose from the table, embracing me without a word. "Oh, Annabelle," she said. "Here I thought maybe you had flipped your lid, or the house was getting to you. I know the truth now; I could feel Christian here with us, even though I couldn't see him. I am just so *sorry.*"

There was something odd about her tone. I stepped back a half step. The way she said that she was sorry sounded more like she felt guilt about something than feeling bad for me. "What on earth would you be sorry for?" I asked her.

Lizzy hesitated for a moment, closing her eyes briefly before shaking her head and smiling at me. "Just that you are going through this." She hugged me again, and I felt bad for thinking that she was acting strange. *Of course, she should be acting strange,* I thought. *Look at what she had just experienced!*

I squeezed her back and smiled, telling her, "It's okay, Lizzy. Love is never something to be sorry for." And that was truly how I felt, in that moment. Later, when it would be time to say goodbye, I wasn't so sure.

Chapter Nineteen

"Hold fast to dreams,
For if dreams die
Life is a broken-winged bird,
That cannot fly."
–**Langston Hughes**

One thing about being involved with a ghost is that you really don't know if you have any privacy or not. I wanted to take some sleeping pills to ensure I went right to sleep that night, but I was afraid Christian was looking over my shoulder and would be disappointed in me. Instead, I drank an entire bottle of wine, something that I have done before, but not in under an hour. I felt so tipsy that I was afraid I'd still be tipsy in my dream.

I drank so much so quickly, for me anyway, that I fell asleep sitting at the kitchen table. The candle that Melissa had relit had finally burned out, the fire I lit in the fireplace for something constructive to do after she and Lizzy left had burned down to embers, and I fell asleep with an empty glass of wine in front of me, my feet propped up on the chair to my right, and my head dropped forward. I am pretty sure I was drooling at least a little.

My head bobbed a bit, and it woke me up, snapping my neck back as my eyes opened. Still my kitchen, still my time; my glass, my candles, my kitchen appliances. Normally when I dream with Christian, I am in his time, and I thought that I was truly awake.

"Shit," I said out loud, thinking I had screwed up my opportunity to be with him.

"What is it, Annabelle?" I heard Christian call from the other room.

"Oh my God. Christian?" I jumped to my feet and ran into the living room. Even in my excitement, I remembered that they had laid his mother out in that room in a homemade casket. I rounded the corner so quickly that I ran right into him, and was elated to find that I ran into a solid body. Well, mostly solid, which was good enough for me. When I hugged him and nuzzled against his neck, I felt his arms wrap around me. The only thing that was missing was a pulse in his neck, but his warmth made up for that. I was worried that he was upset with me for bringing in a medium, and I wanted to talk about it right away. "I'm sorry, Christian, about the medium. You said goodbye to me and then I woke up and didn't see you again, and I..."

Christian silenced me with a kiss, taking away my breath and my worry all at once. "Shh... so many worries you carry around with you. You remind me of myself, so long ago," he told me. "It's okay. It must be confusing. I'm sorry. Melissa was nice. She is concerned about you, and I don't blame her. I never should have let you get involved with me."

"I just don't understand why we can't be together until I'm old and die. I am sure that I can find a spell to let you stay with me. And then you can come with me and we can, I don't know, spend eternity together?" It sounded pretty dumb even as the sentence was coming out of my mouth.

Christian kissed the top of my head and led me to the kitchen table to sit down. He sat right next to me, holding my hand as he spoke. "Annabelle, do you know why I like to sit in the kitchen?"

"Because you used to love to eat?" I guessed, laying my head on his shoulder.

"No. Because almost one hundred and twenty-three years ago, I was born right here. On the kitchen table." I sat up and looked at the table, feeling a little grossed out, and a little bit in awe. He went on, "I was born here, and twenty-three years later, I took my own life in the barn out back. I spend time in here because it reminds me of my death, which reminds me of the ninety-nine years I have spent in limbo, waiting to move on. I don't know what is waiting for me at the end of my hundred years, but I thought that no matter what it is, no matter what darkness lies ahead, it would be worth it, to get away from the constant reminder of what I had done." He stopped talking for a minute, waiting for me to look at him. When I did, he kissed me lightly on the lips before continuing, "Until I met you, I never could imagine wanting contact with the living, because they represented what I could never have. And then you came along and brought love and light back into my life. And now, for the first time, I'm not so eager to move on. But, Annabelle, I have no choice; it is my destiny."

I understood this with my head, but my heart did not want to let go. I pulled away from him and put my head in my shaking hands. "And how much time do we have, Christian?" I asked him.

"I'm not sure. A few days, maybe." He took my hand and put his hand under my chin, making me look at him. "You have to let me go, Annabelle."

"But what if I can make it so you can stay?" I asked, grasping at straws.

"Annabelle, Lillian was a skillful Wiccan. Please don't be hurt by this, but the last time you tried to use the craft to bring me to you, I almost died. Again." He smiled as he said this, but I knew he did not want to experience that again. "And even if you could find a way, I already screwed up my natural life cycle. I don't think that it would be wise for me to do that twice."

I suddenly realized that I might not get to say goodbye to him. "How will I know when your time is up? Will you just disappear? This is totally..." I struggled to find the right words. "This sucks, Christian."

He reached out and wiped tears I hadn't realized had started to fall. Taking my hand, he led me upstairs. We made love, and while there were those crazy streams of light, they didn't seem as bright to me. It was like he was already fading from me, somehow. It was wonderful to be with him, but I couldn't get what he said out of my head. *A few days... let me go.* As I lay in his arms and began to drift back off to "sleep," which was already odd since I was already technically sleeping, I clutched him to me as closely as I could. *This is not enough,* I thought. *I don't want a few more days. I want eternity.* After everything that I had been through with Scott, I wanted to be able to hold on to the person who made me feel safe and loved. Valued.

When I woke up, I was in my own bed. It seemed that Christian had brought me there; I was in bed, with the covers tucked up under my chin. And that is when I figured out the answer to how I could be with Christian for eternity. If he couldn't stay with me, I would stay with him. We would find the light together.

chapter Twenty

"The thought of suicide is a great consolation:
by means of it one gets through many a dark night."
–Nietzsche

I didn't feel like I was killing myself. Now that I knew for sure that there was an afterlife, even if it was still mysterious and scary, I felt like I didn't have to worry about ending my life. I would still be me, and I would get to be with the man I loved. At the time, it seemed perfectly reasonable.

The first hurtle was figuring out how I was going to do it. I could hang myself, like Christian did, but I didn't think that I would have the guts to put a noose around my neck and jump. What if I didn't die, and I swung helplessly around the barn. Christian, of course, would be watching me. Thinking about the horrible night that I brought him back from that moment, I knew there was no way that I would want to put him through that. I would never crash my car or drive off a bridge; for one, I wouldn't want to take the chance of hurting someone else, and two, I wanted to be home so that I had the best chance of being with Christian right away after I died. Pills were an option, though I'd have to get something stronger than ibuprofen and sleeping pills. I could cut my wrists. I did not own a gun, and I had no desire to drown myself. So, my best options seemed like pills and wrists. I did some research on my phone, sitting in the car to get the best internet and using a private browser—old habit from living with someone who went through my phone constantly—and decided that the pills were not the best option. I could pass out; I could vomit them up and do major organ damage; there really was no guarantee that I would die. So, I settled on cutting my wrists, and I decided that to honor Christian, I would do it in the barn, where he died.

I felt oddly peaceful about the whole thing, feeling lucky for the first time that Karma had already been adopted, because I could never do this and leave a dog behind. I thought about calling Nancy, but I didn't know what I would possibly say, so I texted her instead:

Hey sis, just wanted to say hi and I love you. Going off line for a few days, but I will see you soon.

I thought that was actually pretty clever, going off line. And I would see her soon, in her dreams. When I could go into dreams and show her how happy Christian and I were, I knew that she would understand. Maybe I'd even get to see my parents again.

I thought it would be romantic to meet Christian under the moonlight, and I felt antsy with all of the time stretched out before me. Around noon, I walked to Lizzy's, since I knew that she usually took a break from the shop around then for lunch. She once told me that if she ate at the coffee shop every day, she wouldn't be able to fit through the door.

It was a beautiful day, which made me feel even better. The leaves crunched under my feet as I walked through my yard and onto the street, orange and yellow everywhere I looked. The chilly air had that crisp, fresh smell to it. It felt clean. It felt right.

When I got to Lizzy's, she saw me out of her kitchen window and ran out of her house to greet me. She looked worried, and she was. "Oh, Annabelle," she said, hugging me tightly to her, "I had the worst dream about you last night. I went to bed thinking about you and Christian, and everything that has happened, and I dreamt that you killed yourself."

She pulled away from me, and I tried to hide my expression. I spread my arms out and forced a smile onto my face. "I'm just fine, Lizzy, see?" I told her, twirling around in a circle. "Just a crazy dream."

Lizzy smiled back, but still looked distraught. "Yes, here you are. And you seem happy enough," she said. "Come inside, have some lunch with me. I was just making a pepper and onion wrap with tofu."

I followed her in. I was going to miss Lizzy, I knew.

Lizzy had her back to me as she pulled out another wrap and started to scoop the pepper and onion mix into it. "You know, Annabelle, I'm sure Christian is charming and all, but there are flesh and blood men right here in Naples that would make lovely suitors. Nice, handsome, solid men that you can go out to dinner and watch a movie with. Some sweet guy that perhaps even owns a winery?" She turned to me and smiled, waggling her eyebrows up and down for effect. Obviously, she was talking about Ben.

The thought of Ben did make me a little sad. But I knew I was in too deep with Christian to give up now. "Oh yeah? You know someone like that?" I teased her back.

"Come on, Ben is so cute, and he really likes you. He asks about you all the time, Annabelle. He is good-looking and owns a winery, he likes poetry and is nice to little old ladies like me, oh and let's see what else he is—oh, he's alive!" Lizzy put the wrap down in front of me, noticing that I was sitting there frowning. "I'm sorry. I know that this thing with Christian has to play out. I've just been so worried about you, in that house all confused and sad all the time, all alone."

"I'm not alone. And besides, I'm sure Ben would run for the hills if he knew I was sleeping with a ghost." I smiled at her, not wanting to be the cause of any worry or pain for my friend.

"Okay, okay. Maybe he would. Let's talk about something else. How's work going?" she asked me.

"Talk about stressful topics," I told her. "I haven't been able to concentrate on anything, and my editor is getting pissed. I am supposed to be submitting a column twice a week, and I have given him exactly one story. One of these days I am going to run out of money and have to..." I stopped talking, realizing that after that night, I didn't have to ever work again. I smiled.

Have to what, honey?" she asked me.

"Get a different job, I guess. One that I will have to actually go to." I shrugged, not meaning that at all.

Lizzy shook her head and smiled at me. "That may be for the best. Get you out of the house."

I agreed—what else could I say? We chatted for a little bit about how beautiful the fall was this year, and I left when we were finished so that she could head back to the coffee shop. I was a little sad when we said goodbye, and I knew that I'd have to make a visit to her, as well as Nancy. I hoped Ben would understand when Lizzy explained it to him. I certainly couldn't go into his dreams. That would be too weird.

I went home and started to go through my drawers to find something sharp, like a razor blade, for that night. Humming the song "I Passed By Your Window," I felt completely content. I was entirely unaware that Christian had been watching my every move, including when I was in my car and browsing on how to kill myself.

Chapter Twenty-One

"The hunger for love is much more difficult to remove than the hunger for bread."
–Mother Teresa

Love sure does strange things to people. Thankfully, the moon was bright and full, and there were no clouds, so I was able to see pretty well as I entered the aged barn. I stepped up and into the old two-story structure, aware of the musty smell. A few steps in and I realized I was walking all over some sort of small poop. I felt something whiz by my head and realized right away that the poop I was walking on was bat poop. I couldn't imagine what it must have been like for Christian to die in here, I thought, and then realized that I was about to find out. I looked up at the beam that he hung himself from and cold tendrils clawed their way up my back and neck, right to the top of my head. Suddenly freezing, I wanted to get it over with and searched around for a cleanish spot to sit and lean against a wall. Knowing that there must be spiders everywhere, as well as bats and Goddess knows what else, I tried not to look too closely at anything.

I finally just decided, screw it, I'll sit anywhere, and chose a spot where I could see Christian's beam. I thought it might give me courage. I sat there crossed-legged a little while, hands outstretched, palms facing up and resting on my knees, asking the Goddess for forgiveness and guidance. Speaking out loud, I addressed Christian, "Christian, if you can hear me, please know that I love you. If this doesn't work, know that I just want to be with you."

As I reached into my jeans pocket for the razor blade that I found, the wind in the barn picked up. My hands were shaking as I unwrapped the blade from the tissue that I had put it in. All of a sudden, there was a shrill, piercing sound as what seemed like thousands of bats swarmed around me.

"Christian?" I yelled. "I have to do this!" My hair was flying around my face as an old rusty basketball hoop fell from the wall above me and landed feet from where I sat. "Please let me—this is my choice," I said to the windstorm in front of me.

Taking in the deepest breath I could, filling my lungs with life for the last time, I took the blade with my right hand and cut into my left wrist, cutting up my arm until I could no longer take the pain. It surprised me at how badly it stung, and how much blood was coming from the wound. I thought I would be able to take the blade in my left hand to cut my right wrist as well, but my hand was shaking too badly at that point, and the blade was so slippery with blood that I couldn't even grasp it. *It's okay,* I thought. *It may take a while but I will eventually bleed to death.*

In the midst of wind and bats and objects rattling on the walls all around me, I felt completely calm and at peace. "I'm coming, Christian, my love," I whispered, closing my eyes from the storm.

I heard him yelling, but it seemed far away. "Annabelle! No! Annabelle!" The yells were getting closer, and when I opened my eyes, he was right next to me, looking handsome and worried. As my light started to go out, it seemed like his was getting stronger.

"I'm okay, Christian, we'll be together soon," I whispered, looking at the blood running down my arm and into my lap, soaking my jeans and the wood beneath me.

"No! Annabelle, we won't!" Christian grasped my wrist, and in a whirl of wind and debris, he was gone.

"Christian!" I tried to yell, but was losing the energy to do so. I was confused. I didn't know if I had lost consciousness or not. It was hard to tell if I was still in the same place, but I could see him, so I must have been out. Closing my eyes, trying to block out the pain and the noise, I felt myself slip into darkness. Visions of my parents and my sister and me, all together and happy, ran through my mind. I was so happy once, before I married Scott and gave up everything I had once loved. What if I was stuck here, like Christian was, yet without him? The realization dawned on me and it was too late—I felt so weak.

I felt an energy enter the barn, and sure it was Christian, I let myself relax into the weakness. "Annabelle! Annabelle! Oh God, what do I do?" It wasn't Christian. Was it my mother?

"Mom?" I asked, not sure if I said it out loud or not. "Mom?!" Elated and scared, I opened my eyes.

Not my mother. Not Christian. My eyes slowly opened and there was Lizzy, covered in my blood and holding a towel on my wrist. When she saw my eyes open, she cried out with relief. "Oh, thank God. Annabelle. Oh my God." She started to cry, and so did I, because I knew my plan was flawed, and dumb, and I had failed. I looked down to my wrist and thought about every stupid thing that had happened over the past few months, and about how I had just tried to kill myself to be with someone that I could never be with, and I felt a hopelessness seep into my bones. I closed my eyes and drifted away, to a place where Christian was waiting for me with open arms. This time, I knew that we were in my dream, and I was certain that it was not forever.

By the time they released me from the hospital, it was late the next night. Lizzy signed me out; we lied and said she was my aunt. I told the doctors that I was afraid of my husband and panicked, thinking that suicide was better than being with him. I promised to call the counseling number that they gave me. It turned out that my cuts were not all that deep—I guess I didn't pick the best method to kill myself after all. I probably would have died eventually, but I would have needed iron willpower to lie there in bat poop and slowly die, without ever calling for help.

On the ride home, I finally had the courage to look at Lizzy and thank her. "Lizzy, you saved my life. I am so embarrassed." I put my head in my hands, wincing when I lifted my wrapped wrist. "How did you even know to come to me?"

Keeping one hand on the wheel, Lizzy reached over and put her other hand on my shoulder. "Well, lucky for both of us, I wasn't feeling well and decided to call it an early night from the coffee shop," she told me. "I fell asleep on the couch, actually, and that's when Christian came to me in my dream. He scared the shit out of me, that's for sure, shaking me and yelling at me that you were in the barn and that you were going to die. I don't think I remember actually waking up and running up to the barn, but I must have, because I was very much awake when I saw you lying there."

I was mortified, but also grateful. "Thank you so much, Lizzy. I'm sure working in the circus was nothing compared to living next to me. I don't know how to ever thank you."

"Well, you can start by promising me to never, ever, ever try to do anything like that again. What were you thinking, Annabelle?"

"I am an asshole. I knew it when I started to pass out, but it was too late. I thought if I killed myself, I could be with Christian. I thought I'd still be able to see you and my sister when you dream. I thought that I could have it all, but I know now that it just isn't possible. I'm losing him and there is nothing I can do." I started to cry again, something I couldn't seem to control any longer.

Lizzy pulled the car over and put it in Park, so that she could look at me. She looked right into my eyes and said, "You will get through this, and we will do it together. Stop thinking that you're alone, Annabelle. Learn to lean a little." She gave my hand a quick squeeze.

Why will we do it together? The thought hit me as Lizzy put her hand on the shifter. I must have had the thought out loud, because she did not put the car back in Drive. A minute passed, and we sat there in silence, staring into the dark. It suddenly seemed odd to me that Lizzy—a stranger, really—has been so involved and concerned with my life.

There was something else, too. She seemed too invested in my happiness. My safety. "It's not that I'm not grateful," I began. "I am. So grateful. And I know that I put a lot on you, as a new friend, coming to your home and talking about the ghost in mine. But sometimes, you seem a little too worried about me."

Lizzy closed her eyes. Took a deep breath. "Oh, Annabelle, I should have told you from the beginning."

"Told me what?" Goose bumps broke out on my arms.

"Lillian was—well, is—my grandmother."

"What?!" I was confused. "Lillian, the witch who put a spell on Christian, is your grandmother?"

"My real name is not Elizabeth. It is Lizbeth, which was Lillian's middle name as well as my mother's. I decided to use Lizzy and never use my birth name, because I feel—oh, God—I feel cursed right along with poor Christian. What my grandmother did to him is unforgiveable. She was a vindictive woman, and he has been suffering for so long. I couldn't face using her name once she died." Tears fell onto her shirt. Her aging hands trembled on the steering wheel.

Silence again.

I was not sure what to feel. A part of me was angry at the secret, and a little afraid, as well. Could Lizzy somehow be as evil as her grandmother? Or even as powerful? I looked over at her sagging shoulders and bent head, tears falling on her lap, and all of that fear and anger was replaced with an understanding. Lizzy was not evil, and I realized why she was so concerned for me. She felt guilty. That was a lot of years of guilt to feel, and it wasn't even hers.

I took her shaking hand. "Lizzy, look at me." She did. "That makes sense. Your grandmother... she was not a good person. But you are. And none of this is your fault."

Lizzy smiled finally, and gave me a brief family history. After Christian's death, Lillian became more of a wild woman than ever. She started to sleep around, and she became pregnant by Robert Miller, the man who Christian spotted her with. When he was drafted for the war, she had his baby, a little girl, and she named her Christine Lisbeth. It seems that she wanted a constant reminder of what she did, as it made her feel powerful. When Christine's father died in the war, Lillian became a recluse, sitting in her tiny house across the street from Christian's farmhouse, waiting for him to show himself to her. But he never did. When Christine was just ten, she found Lillian with her wrists slit."

"Oh my gosh, that is horrible."

"It was actually a blessing," Lizzy told me. "My mother felt like the curse was lifted, and that finally some happiness would be allowed into her life. A family from town adopted her, and she lived a pretty normal life. When she passed and I retired from circus life, I decided to move back here, keep an eye on the place. And when I saw you move in, all alone, I was worried for you. I knew that Christian's spirit was still stuck here, and you seemed so alone. I'm so sorry," she told me again.

I reached out and wiped the tears from Lizzy's cheeks. "I love you, Lizzy. And I love that you have been watching out for me. And for Christian. This all makes sense now."

Lizzy smiled. She let out a breath, seemingly more relaxed than I had seen her yet. She put the car in Drive and pulled back onto the road, singing softly to herself.

We were quiet for a few minutes, just the hum of Lizzy's tune, when she suddenly stopped and took a deep breath in, as if she were shocked or frightened. "What is it?" I asked her, my own nerves on edge.

Lizzy's grip tightened a bit on the steering wheel. "Do you remember when you told me about how you and Christian were able to meet in your dream? Like he could slip right in there?"

"Yes," I answered simply, worried about where she was going with this.

"I'm sure it's nothing. I'm sure it's just my overactive imagination or old family guilt, but I have dreamt about my grandmother," she told me, as if making another confession.

"That's probably normal," I told her, wanting to abate any more bad feelings that she was having. "Many people have dreams of deceased family, even if they were not, um, close."

Lizzy nodded, not seeming to be pacified. Her knuckles were white from holding on so tight. "Yes but, I have had dreams that seemed more like memories. I have seen Christian fall from the rafter, and I have seen it from her perspective. And lately, I have dreamt of her, as a young woman, in my own house, telling me to mind my business." Lizzy stopped talking and looked over at me with wide eyes.

"Well, first of all," I told her, with a little bit of attitude to lighten the mood, "I'm glad that you didn't 'mind your business,' because you saved my life. And second of all, if your *grandmother* is walking around people's dreams, maybe she can come into mine and we can have a little chat about what she did to Christian."

I don't know if that helped her to feel better or not, but Lizzy smiled, shoulders relaxing a bit. "You're right," she said, wiggling her fingers to let the blood flow again. "I'm not about to be bossed around by someone I never even met. If she pops into my sleep again, I'll tell her to make like a tree and leaf me alone."

Lizzy always had a way of turning the darkness sunny again, and I was grateful for her humor. We laughed the rest of the way home, talking about the cheesiest ways to tell off a ghost.

As we pulled into my driveway, Lizzy asked what I was going to be doing that night, and asked me if I wanted her to stay with me. I leaned over and hugged her, but declined. "It's okay, I'll be okay. I've got to try to reach Christian," I told her.

"Annabelle," she protested, smile fading from her face, but I cut her off.

"Lizzy, it's okay. I was reading over the research I did on Christian, and I found the date that he killed himself. It was one hundred years ago tonight. If he is right, Christian will be gone by tomorrow. I have to say goodbye."

Chapter Twenty-Two

"The song is ended, but the melody lingers on."
–Irving Berlin

Lizzy insisted she walk me inside, and I didn't argue with her. I was tired, and embarrassed, and really sore. My body was exhausted, and my mind was, too, and I knew that it wasn't over yet. I would still have to see Christian once I fell asleep. And I also knew that I would likely have to say goodbye to him, as well. I felt like my heart couldn't take much more pain. Lizzy and I sat at the kitchen table and chatted for a few minutes before I walked her to the door and, hugging her tightly, said good night.

"Thank you so much," I told her, feeling like those words were so small for what I really meant to say.

Lizzy looked worried when I pulled away from our hug. She held up her pointer finger and jabbed it in the air toward my chin, like my grandmother used to do when she knew that I was up to no good. "Don't do anything crazy," she said. And with a last smile, she left me alone.

I turned to face the kitchen and realized that the same soft music that Christian had played for me before was playing on the radio. I was sure that the radio was off when I first got home. I felt like Christian was beckoning me to him, so I said to the empty room, "I'm coming, my love. Sleep should find me easy tonight."

It turned out that sleep did not find me easily. I tossed and turned; I couldn't get comfortable. First, I was cold, followed by being too hot. My wrist was killing me, and I promised myself (and Lizzy) that I would not take anything stronger than some ibuprofen. Every time I closed my eyes, I saw bats swooping down at me, tasting my blood, getting tangled in my hair. I kept feeling under my legs to be sure there was no bat poop there; I swore I could feel it under my skin, the way it turned to dust as soon as I touched it, the little pellets sticking to my sweaty legs. Once I did start to drift off, I thought about Christian's mother, lying in the parlor, the stench of death leaking out of her coffin and rousing me from my sleep. I thought I heard her calling my name. *"Annabelle,"* she called in a singsong motherly way. *"Come play with us, Annabelle."* I covered my ears, tears rolling down my face, salt getting in my mouth. Until finally, finally I felt Christian sit down on my bed by my side, hushing me and stroking my hair. I guess I finally fell asleep. I unclamped my ears and was relieved to hear only his voice.

As soon as I looked up at him, I felt so ashamed by what I had done. Christian took my hand and brought it to his lips, which felt so soft and warm. When he lifted up my hand and saw my wrist, covered in the bandage, he pulled me to him and held me for what seemed an eternity. After a while, he pulled away, and I could see the tears slowly falling down his face. "I am so sorry, Annabelle," he told me.

"You're sorry?" I managed to laugh at that, wiping tears of my own. "It is me who is sorry. I don't know what I was thinking. I didn't want to lose you and thought that if I died, too, then we would be together. I'm such an idiot."

Christian smiled at that, and said, "You forget, my dear Annabelle, that I'm an idiot, too. You know that I took my own life, and you know that I did it over love."

After all we had been through, that made me a little jealous. I asked him, "Do you still love her, Christian?"

He took my hand gently in his, kissed it once more, and said, "No, Annabelle. That was a lifetime ago—that was a few of my lifetimes ago. I was in love with a woman who did not exist. I thought I knew her, but I did not. But I know now that I was wrong, and foolish. Lillian was not right for me, yet she was with me. We were neighbors, and I was with her always. I did not even know that she practiced wicca, and I spent much of my life watching over her. If I have learned anything, it's that people fool themselves into falling in love because it's what they think they want."

I winced a little at this, and he quickly went on. "You, Annabelle, are the perfect woman for me and I love you with all my heart, but you are in your time. My heart breaks at this, but we just cannot be."

I pulled Christian down to the bed and he climbed under the sheets with me. We talked a bit about time and circumstance, and about how he was no longer regretful that he took his own life because he finally found love. He told me that I should move on, that there was another fate that awaited me. I shook my head at this, burying myself as deeply into his body as I could. "I will never love anyone as I love you," I told him.

"And I will be grateful for all eternity that I tasted that love," he told me, and I closed my eyes. Lying on his chest, I wanted to stay up all night to talk with him, to soak up whatever essence that he would leave behind.

I wish I could tell you we talked until a great burst of light appeared, and that we kissed as I walked him to the brink of that light and watched him walk away in peace. I wish I could tell you that Christian found that light because of our love. I wish I could tell you I knew.

But sometime during the next few hours, I fell into a comfortable sleep. And when I awoke, he was simply, undeniably, gone.

The house felt empty. I could feel his void as well as I could feel his body in my dreams. It was still dark out, but the crickets were starting their morning chants, and I knew that daylight would come soon enough.

Sadness crept over me as I pulled myself out of bed and forced myself to get up and face whatever awaited me. Christian's words about my fate rang in my ears, but I felt that I knew that my fate was with him, and with him gone, I would surely perish. I smiled, thinking it ironic that I was becoming the lonely poet.

As I walked past the parlor and into the kitchen, I knew it was time for me to leave this house, as well. So much had happened here: Scott almost raped me. I tried to kill myself. I lost the man I love. My breathing suddenly felt funny, like I was trapped in a dark well and couldn't find my way out. I tried to sit on a chair at the table but ended up on the floor, my vision a blur of dots and tears. I must have hit my head on something as I passed out.

What I saw as I passed out—or what I didn't see—enveloped me in comfort. Darkness. No feeling, no sadness, nothing. I wanted to remain in that space forever.

"Annabelle?" I heard a voice calling my name, pulling me out of that pit.

"Mom?" I answered. No, that couldn't be. My mother was dead. Yet she called to me again.

"Annabelle. You need to wake up." It *was* her. I knew it was.

"Mom? Mom!" I called back to her, opening my eyes and looking around the room. But she was not there. I pulled myself up off the floor and onto the kitchen chair. I thought about how Christian was born on the table, and I rubbed my hand over the surface like it was a baby. I had no idea what to do next, or how to go on, and these were my thoughts when I looked up and noticed a bottle of wine on my table.

I felt cold suddenly as I realized I had definitely not put that bottle there. I was pretty sure Lizzy hadn't, either, since I know she thinks I have been drinking too much. I did not recognize the bottle, but I did notice the name of the winery on the label. It was from Ben's winery, right in town.

I wanted to think that Christian somehow procured it from the spirit realm and left it for me as a sign. A sign for what? I wondered. Perhaps to move on, perhaps to live out some unknown fate that he thought I was missing out on. Or perhaps it was just a gift from Ben, who may have heard I was in the hospital, and somehow dropped it off while I was asleep. Slowly I reached across the table, lifted the bottle, and found a little white note, folded up under the bottle. As I opened it up, another icy chill traveled up my spine, and it wasn't a happy one. I read it out loud: *"I asked around town to see who you've been hanging out with. I knew there must be someone else. I talked to a charming man who owns a winery, and I know how much you love your wine. When I mentioned your name, he was awfully defensive of you. I knew you must have been cheating to leave me. I hope you enjoy this bottle, darling, as the winery and its handsome proprietor won't be around for long."*

The note wasn't signed, but I would recognize Scott's writing anywhere. "What the fuck, Scott?" I fumed out loud. I grabbed my cell and ran outside.

Lizzy picked up on the second ring, even though I knew she must be sleeping. "Are you okay?" she asked as a greeting.

My words came out in one jumbled string as I told her about the note that I found under the bottle of wine from Ben's winery. "Call Ben, let him know that Scott is out of his mind," I told her. "I'm headed over there now."

I didn't give her time to tell me not to go. I hung up my cell and got in my car, leaving a wake of frosty leaves blowing out from under my car as I sped to the other side of town.

Chapter Twenty-Three

"Some men, like a tiled house, are long before they take fire, but once on flame there is no coming near to quench them."
–Thomas Fuller

The flames were barely visible when I pulled into the Grapes of Wrath Winery, which was just outside of town. Throwing my Cherokee into Park before it was even fully stopped, I ran toward the building. I had been there only once, but I remembered from the tour that the building that was on fire was the main tasting room, and Ben lived upstairs. I didn't even know if Ben knew what was happening, because everything was quiet. Everything except for a sound that I can only describe as a light rain, and it was getting louder. I yelled up toward the second-floor window to try to rouse Ben, but my shouts seemed to go unheard.

"Ben! Ben!" I shouted over and over, but as far as I could tell in the darkness, it was only me and the growing flames of the building in front of me. I ran to the back of the building, opposite from where the flames were, and saw Scott's car, the red of the Corvette, glowing in the moonlight like some demonic symbol.

"Oh shit," I said, running toward the back door. I tried the doorknob, and it was unlocked, so I shoved open the door and ran inside. The fire still seemed small and on the other side of the building, but the smoke was already overwhelming. I pulled my T-shirt up over my mouth and searched for the stairs, my eyes stinging as I made my way through the downstairs hallway, past the offices that I remembered from the tour, and to the stairs that led to Ben's place.

At the top of the landing was a small hallway with different doors that led to different parts of the apartment. Before Ben moved up there, the second floor was used for offices and storage. I tried the first door, and it was locked, but I started banging on the door and the walls and yelling for Ben. I came to the second door, and it was unlocked, so I slowly pushed it open, afraid of what I might find. The lights were off, but the sun was starting to rise and let some light in through the window. I entered Ben's apartment through what seemed to be a game room—a pool table sat uncovered on one side of the massive room, a couch and small bar on the opposite wall—tiptoeing past the table and through the next door, which was open a crack. I don't know why I was suddenly afraid to call out, when just moments earlier I was calling Ben's name like a lunatic, but I opened that next door as quietly as I could, and what I saw was Scott, kneeling on the floor, a fire of his own in his eyes, hands behind his head. Just feet from him was Ben, holding a shotgun, pointing it at Scott's face. On the floor next to Scott was a red container that stank like gasoline.

"What in the hell—*Scott, what are you doing*?" I yelled at him, so mad I could have hit him with Ben's shotgun.

I stepped toward him and realized that his nose was bleeding. Ben must have struck him, and I was glad. When I got closer to Scott, he tried to stand up, but then glanced at the gun and stayed where he was. "Annabelle, you have to get out of that house," he told me, as if he were my father and I his teenage daughter. "I don't know what you are doing with this guy, but it's time to stop this and come home."

I laughed. "First of all, you don't get to tell me what to do. I left, Scott—you lost that right. And second, *this guy* is my friend, and I'm a lot safer with my friends than with my so-called protector." I was so mad that I almost forgot the building was on fire downstairs, but the smoke that followed me up the stairs was a shocking reminder. "Oh my God, Ben, your place is on fire," I said, stating the obvious.

"Get up," Ben told Scott, keeping the shotgun pointed in his direction. Ben pointed to the door and followed Scott through, and the three of us made our way down the stairs and into the smoke-filled hallway. As we neared the exit door and stepped outside into the fresh air, the noise was deafening and confusing. The piercing sound combined with the smell of the burning gas was overwhelming, and I sank to the ground and covered my ears. A moment later, someone was standing right in front of me, grabbing my shoulders and trying to lift me up. I opened my eyes and saw Lizzy, and with the sun coming up behind her, she had the aura of an angel.

"My guardian angel," I told her, as I let her help me stand up. I looked around and realized the sounds I heard were fire trucks and cop cars. Of course, Lizzy had dialed 911. I felt like an idiot for not doing that myself.

"Always running toward the trouble," Lizzy told me, as if she could read my mind. She smiled and nodded toward Ben, who was talking to the police. I noticed for the first time that he was wearing only boxers, his back and legs strong and tan. "But that one isn't trouble, he's one of the good ones."

I shook my head. "He must think I'm a flake. I can't believe this is happening," I said, as I looked around to survey the damage in the rising light. The building was okay, some destruction, but nothing that couldn't be fixed. Scott was being put into a cop car, and when I looked over at him and our eyes met, I felt nothing but sadness for what he had become. When the car finally drove away with Scott inside, I was so relieved that I started to cry.

Lizzy and I sat at a picnic table and watched the sun come up as Ben finished up with the police and the fire crew. She had some blankets in her car—of course she did—and she wrapped one around Ben's shoulders and shared one with me. When Ben finally walked over to us, I was embarrassed all over again. "Ben, I am so sorry. I don't know what made him think that we were together. He's crazy," I said.

Ben smiled and sat down next to us, sandwiching me between him and Lizzy. "When he found me working earlier and asked me if I knew you and where you were, I didn't know who he was, but he seemed so angry. I was probably a little too defensive of you, but I was worried because he seemed so hostile. I may have told him if he wanted you, he'd have to go through me." Ben paused and looked at me, the color rising on his already tanned face. I smiled, and he continued, "He just stormed off and I figured that was the end of it. I tried to call you to warn you that he may be headed your way, but I couldn't get through."

He probably tried to call when I was at the hospital, I figured, which made me all too aware of the bandage around my wrist. He seemed to notice it, too, as I tried to wrap the blanket around my arm. "Are you okay, Annabelle?" he asked me, surprise and concern in his voice.

"It was an accident," I told him. "I-I don't really want to relive the gory details right now," I said, looking at Lizzy for support.

Lizzy took my cue. "Well, handsome," she said, getting up from the table and putting her arms around Ben for a hug. "I have had my fill of drama for a few days. Gotta go back to the shop." She hugged me, too, and I realized that I didn't want to leave my new friends. I didn't want to leave the town or my home.

After we said goodbye to Lizzy, Ben offered me some coffee, which I declined, but I promised to return later to help clean up some of the damage. "I am so sorry about all of this," I told him.

"That's alright, not your fault that your ex is an asshole. Plus, I'm sure my response played a small part in his outburst," he laughed. "He sure doesn't like guns, though. Are you sure you're okay?"

"I think so. It's been a rough few days," I told him, thinking that was the understatement of the year. "I'll be back later on to help out."

Ben smiled, eyes meeting mine. "Nah, you're going to be busy today," he told me.

That made me laugh, as my social calendar was wide open at that moment. Before I could figure out how to answer that, he put his hand up and told me he'd be right back. I was suddenly nervous, wondering what on earth he meant. I wasn't ready for a date, an adventure, or plans of any sort. When he disappeared into the building, I took a deep breath, but before I could assume too much, he was walking back toward me, cell phone in his hand.

Opening his messenger app, Ben's smile was wide, reaching his eyes as he clicked on a photo. "You know how they say Karma's a bitch?" he asked. I nodded, thinking of course of the cocker that I felt like I had lost. "Well, it's true, and she's all yours if you still want her."

He handed me his phone, and my confusion turned to joy as I was staring at a picture of the dog, Karma. "Wait, what do you mean?" I asked, hope filling my heart.

"I got this message just before the fire. Turns out that one of Karma's new owners is actually allergic and had to bring her back. Sad, but it seems like a touch of fate?"

Oh, yes, it was! I threw my arms around Ben, and he hugged me back until I pulled away, embarrassed.

"Sorry, I get a little overzealous sometimes," I told him shyly.

That laugh again. "It's okay, Annabelle. That's exactly the right reaction when it comes to this girl. She is really sweet, and housebroken, and I think you'll love her."

Now it was my turn to laugh. My life has had some crazy turns in those past few weeks, and this seemed to be exactly what I needed to happen to help me move on and heal. "Oh, I think that I already do love her," I told him

Suddenly worried, I realized I had never owned a dog before, and maybe the shelter wouldn't adopt to me. It had never occurred to me the first time that I went there, but now it made sense that there would be an adoption process. I shared this with Ben, who put me at ease right away.

"Remember when I said I'd put in a good word for you?" he asked me. "I let them know that you were Lizzy's friend, and everyone knows that she's got a great sense about people..."

I cut him off. "Yeah, but she's only even known me a short time," I reminded him.

"Annabelle. You write for a newspaper and had your own column about shelter pets. Robert already knew who you were, stating that you have gotten more pets adopted than anyone he knows. You're in, don't worry about it."

I wanted to hug him again, but stopped myself. "Well. A job perk that I never even considered. Thanks. Now, I gotta go. Lots to do before my new best friend comes home!"

We had an awkward goodbye—a half hug, half cheek kiss, and I got in my Cherokee and drove off, watching him in my rearview mirror as I pulled out of the winery. I shook my head, those pesky tears running down my cheeks again. Christian was gone. Forever this time. My heart hurt, but I felt like life was right somehow, like I'd been upside down for a while and things were going right-side up finally. I thought I would feel lonely, but I didn't, as if my new friends and now Karma were all here to help me recover.

I pulled over on the side of the road and grabbed a tissue from my glove box. I was tired of crying, ready for a fresh start. "I'm coming, sweetheart," I said, directing my thoughts to Karma, who was waiting for me as I waited for her. She would be the one to rescue me, and I knew I was right not to get another dog, as she was the one all along. I looked into the sky, not sure if I was talking to Christian, or my parents, or whatever force out there that was responsible for giving us what we need at that exact right moment. Not the moment that we *think* is right, but the one that is *actually* right.

"Thank you," I whispered, and I chucked my tissues unceremoniously on the passenger floor. No more crying for me, as I had a dog to pick up.

Chapter Twenty-Four

"You don't drown by falling in the water; you drown by staying there."

–Edwin Louis Cole

And that's the story.

As I sit at my kitchen table trying to figure out what to do, I think about all that has happened to me since I moved into this house. It's been only a few months, but the sorrow of losing Christian has already lifted. Maybe it's because I knew all along that we couldn't really be together, but it seems like it ended the way it was supposed to end. I wish I was with him when he left, though, so I knew what happened to him. I like to imagine him walking through some glowing white light, and I have to let go of the fact that I won't ever see him again to find out. For a few nights after he left, I dreamt of him, but I always knew that I was dreaming my own dream, and that he wasn't really there.

Karma, of course, has helped to heal me and fill my heart with love. She is my best friend. It's like she's been here with me forever. She lays at my feet, golden fur glistening in the sunshine that streams through the windows, snoring softly. When I picked her up at the shelter that day, she came running to me like I was her long-lost mommy, like it was me whom she had been waiting for all these years. Whenever I am sad, usually reminiscing about Christian or my parents—which I have done a lot lately—I sit on the floor and she comes to me, puts her head to my forehead, and looks into my eyes. I swear she is telling me that everything is alright, and I believe her.

Lizzy and I have become even closer. It feels like she has become part friend, part sister, part mother to me. I know that she is concerned about me because I haven't really left my house since the fire at Ben's winery, but she has come over a few times, and she even brought Ben here one night to have dinner with us. We have kept the conversation light, though, and that is something I appreciate. The cuts on my wrist have almost healed, which is one reason why I haven't wanted to leave home. I don't want people to assume that I tried to commit suicide. My life is so full now, with Karma and my friends, that I can hardly match that version of myself up with who I am now. When I think about what I had done, about how I fell for a ghost after only meeting with him a few times in my dreams, falling so hard for him that I was willing to end my life to be with him, it seems crazy. Improbable. But then I remember his soft touch, the way he looked at me, gentle and with such love, and I realize that I needed that softness so badly I was willing to die for it.

Miraculously—and I mean that—my editor loved my column and wants me to do an entire series. He knew, of course, the rough details about Scott trying to burn down the winery, and he thinks that I can really help women in similar situations to gain strength and courage. I am happy to do that. I don't want to be a poster child for abused women, but it will give me fulfillment to help others like me. Well, almost like me. I will keep my love affair with Christian out of the public eye. I also got permission to start my shelter column back up, a way to keep the good karma rolling for these animals.

Nancy read my column and called me a few weeks ago and seemed really proud of me. Now that Christian is gone and Scott is in jail—for the time being, anyway—I invited her out to see me. She will be here in another week, so I have to make sure a room is ready for her.

I pull my sweater around me as I put more logs on the fire. Although spring is just around the corner, nights are still cold. All that has been running through my mind for weeks has been what to do with my life: sell the house and start fresh some place else, or stay here and live with the constant reminders of all that has happened. The song on my mind for days has been "Should I Stay or Should I Go" by The Clash, and it s getting on my nerves. Both the constant replay in my head, and the indecision of what to do. If only there was a sign, a little help from above.

I find myself lost in the flames of the fireplace, and the sound of my phone buzzing with a new text message startles me. I think back—always thinking back to Christian—of my first days in the house when my phone lost service, then power, then turned back on again, and remind myself that it's not him.

A text:

Poetry reading tonight at Lizzy's. You down?

It's from Ben. I smile and stare at the flames for a moment before answering.

I have nothing to read. Do you?
Heck no. Turns out I don't have the guts to read poetry out loud. We can go heckle the poets tonight.

For the first time since before Christian left, I laugh. A real, deep down belly laugh, the kind my mom used to call her happy laugh. And not because I want to go, but because of the gift of laughter that I was not expecting. I type back:

Sure. As long as you promise to spike the coffee. And maybe one day you can read that poem for me.

We'll see 😊

Smiling at his answer, I put my phone down and look around the kitchen. I remember that Christian was born in this room, and I put my hand on the table. "You said to move on," I say, not really thinking that he can hear me but saying it just in case. "I will always love you." I look over at the radio, waiting for it to start playing some old-fashioned love song, but of course, there is nothing. My phones dings, and there is an email from Ben.

The email was short: "Since I don't have the courage to read poetry out loud, I figured you may as well have your very own copy 😊 Don't be too harsh. -Ben"

I sigh and open the attachment, and against my better judgement, I can feel a smile creep to my lips. *Another poet*, I think. *Just what I need to tug on my heartstrings*. The title of Ben's poem is the name of his winery. Interesting.

Grapes of Wrath

The grapes from these hills run through my veins as they ran through the vines on the mound where my father is buried.

These vines, these grapes, this wine. This body.

The ground, the soil, is fertile. But to whose fate will till such land?

The loss in these vines eats at my soul, drinks my blood, is poured over the soil.

Red, purple, blue, burgundy. The shade of spilled blood, the color of what fills the glass before me.

The grapes from these hills, will they ever run dry?

Well geez, it's no wonder the guy drinks bourbon.

I get up from the table and close the fireplace flue, shutting the glass doors to starve the flame that just moments ago I stoked. Karma is laying on her back, belly up, gazing at me as if wondering why on earth I would think of leaving this comfortable spot. I had planned on sitting right here, in this rocking chair, drinking wine and cuddling Karma. But it looks like I have a poetry reading to attend.

Epilogue

"Time, like an ever-rolling stream,
Bears all its sons away;
Thy fly forgotten, as a dream
Dies at the opening day."
—Isaac Watts, from *Our God, Our Help*

It is cold outside, and the slush on the ground soaks through my sneakers as I finish up my walk. I have been thinking about Christian a lot these past few weeks, as I prepare to move back into the house. Even though the arthritis in my hands make them ache during weather like this, I grab a hold of the For Rent sign that is outside on the front lawn, and tug it out of the ground, pulling up frozen earth as I yank with my whole body to get the stakes out of the ground.

It's a good thing that I haven't yet rented the house again since the previous tenants moved out six months ago. They have been here for fifty years, since I first decided to rent it out, not having the heart to sell when I moved in with Ben right before our wedding. It feels like a lifetime ago. In many ways, it was a lifetime ago. All those years, the family who lived in the house begged me to sell, but I just couldn't. Too many memories. And it seems to have worked out perfectly, because I can't bear to stay at the winery with Ben gone.

We had the best fifty years of marriage that anyone could ever hope for. The winery was an enormous success, with the way Naples has boomed as an artist's town. We were so happy, and our kids had a great childhood. Ben Jr. is now going to take over the winery, and even though he told me that I should stay on the property, it just feels so empty without Ben that I can't stand it. It is time for me to come home. My daughter was given the name Lizzy, named after her "Aunt Lizzy," who is now the first official person to be put into a biodegradable urn and planted at the Grapes of Wrath Winery, up on the hill, overlooking the fields of grapes. My daughter is an artist herself, living in Canandaigua with her girlfriend. They own a tattoo shop that they are partners in. She could convince me to get only one tattoo: a tiny butterfly on the inside of my left wrist. It covers up those old scars and is a symbol for life after death. It is a constant reminder that we do move on.

I look up at the house, and at the fields beyond. The barn is gone now; we had to have it taken down because of its state of disrepair. It was a sad day for me, as the fire department came and burned it for us, and all of those memories came flooding back to me. Christian, Lizzy, how I almost died. But Ben was by my side, with his arm around me, and my kids were there to make sure that I was okay. They didn't want me to watch it burn, but I had to. As the beam that I called Christian's beam fell and burned, I cried fresh tears for the pain that he suffered. The worst part about burning the barn was explaining to Karma's gravesite why her forever view would be changing. Once she passed, I never got another dog. I couldn't bear to lose another being that I loved so much. She was with me for fourteen years, living until she was just shy of her twentieth birthday, giving me the best love I could ask for until she went to sleep one night and didn't wake up.

I am lucky because I have had a lifetime of wonderful memories to outweigh the heartbreaking ones. The good memories don't replace the sad ones, though. Those memories will never be replaced, just as Christian will live on in my heart until I am gone.

One night, just a few weeks ago, I dreamt I was back in this house, and when I walked into the kitchen, a song played on the old radio. The song, "A Change is Gonna Come," was a cover of the original by Sam Cooke, sung by Brian and Thomas Owens. The lyrics struck me, and I knew that this was no ordinary dream.

> *It's been a time that I thought*
> *Lord this couldn't last for very long, oh now*
> *But somehow I thought I was still able to try to carry on*
> *It's been a long, long time coming*
> *But I know a change is gonna come*
> *Oh, yes it is.*

I had my eyes closed and when I opened them, Ben was there at the table, sitting right where Christian sat during our first dream together. The once familiar cold chills ran up my spine. "Ben? What's going on?" I asked him. I had not dreamed about this house since I left to be with Ben.

He rose to embrace me, telling me he loves me. "You are my entire world, Annabelle. You mean everything to me. You have made me inexplicably happy for an entire fifty years. An entire lifetime."

"I love you, too, darling. Let's talk more in the morning," I said, taking his hand in mine.

Ben sat down at the table and asked me to sit next to him. "No, Annabelle, I can't," he said, a tear running down his face and plunking down on the table in front of me.

"What do you mean, you can't? What's wrong?" I asked him, confused. I knew that Ben hadn't been feeling well, but the doctor said he was just run-down and needed to take it easy.

"It was my heart. And it was my time to go. I'm so sorry, Annabelle, but I am gone." He stroked my face with his hand, and I shook him off.

"No. Ben, no. You can't leave me. You are my happily ever-after. You can't go," I begged him, sobbing now in his arms. I moved over to sit on his lap, burrowing my head under his chin, saying "I love you," over and over.

I felt his lips kiss the top of my head, and I closed my eyes. "Goodbye, my love," he whispered.

I opened my eyes to look at him, but he was already gone, and I was awake. Frantically I sat up in bed, and there he was, lying as still as death, looking peaceful. There was still color in his face, but when I reached out and touched his cheek, it was already cold. Ben was dead, and even as I went through the motions of checking his pulse and calling 911 for help, I knew that he had passed before he came to me in my sleep.

"Carve your name on hearts, not tombstones. A legacy is etched into the minds of others and the stories they share about you."
–Shannon Alder

I am still sleepy from my nap. I seem to spend more time napping lately than I do being awake. The sun streams through the curtains of my bedroom, and even though my head is propped up on pillows, I struggle to sit up. Lyrics from so long ago run through my mind today: *"I passed by your window in the cool of the night. The lilies were watching so still and so white..."*

Today is the seventeenth anniversary of Ben's death. How did the time go by so fast? I take a few deep breaths and force myself to get out of bed. Slowly, with my cane always by my side, I walk out to the kitchen. I am glad to be alone today; my kids mean well, but they really shouldn't be sitting around all day with an old woman like myself. I have enjoyed mostly good health, but a little cold causes them to come running. I sent them away this morning, promising that I would call them and the home aide that they hired if I do so much as cough.

I finally reach the kitchen sink and stare out the window a moment, wondering how, with all of this beauty, anyone can ever feel alone. A momma deer cautiously looks around before bringing her babies into the yard to eat some apples. My eyes readjust and I am looking now at my own reflection, which looks back at me in wonder. Deep lines etch my face. I have kept my hair long, but it is all gray now, and I still squint sometimes, even though I have been wearing glasses for many years.

Something in the reflection behind me catches my eye, and I see a wineglass on the table, which is impossible because my doctor made me promise to stop drinking about two years ago. Imagine, telling an old woman that she has to save her liver. Is that a chill I feel on my neck? I turn around, half expecting to see Christian or perhaps Ben, but there is no one there, and the table is empty. My eyes must be playing tricks on me. That has been happening a lot lately, seeing things that aren't there. My dreams, mostly mundane and lacking the excitement that I used to find in them, have even changed lately, becoming more colorful and vivid.

I walk, slowly and carefully, over to my favorite chair at the table and sit down. How I wish to have someone to talk with. I look around and my eyes settle on the sunflower painting, so long the source of a reason to argue with Scott. I smile. I had won that battle.

I am tired suddenly, as if I don't even have the energy to rise and walk to the next room to lie down. My hand rubs the table mindlessly in front of me, and as always, I think of Christian. I have been so lucky to have had two loves in my life. Christian, and my dear, sweet Ben. I close my eyes to think about them, indulging in the memories that flood my mind. I even think about Scott, in our early days, when we both still had such love in our hearts for each other.

My head feels heavy now, and I lay it on the table. I feel such peace. I can hear voices; they sound far away but are coming closer. "Christian?" I mumble, "Is that you?" Voices swirl around my head. First Christian, saying, "It's me, Annabelle," and then Ben, "My love, you're going to be safe." And perhaps the happiest mixture of all, Nancy, my mother, and Lizzy, together telling me that they are there to walk me home. They are giggling. Happy. Is that a bark? It is a bark; my Karma is there too!

There is warmth on my back, a light pushing its way past the shadows and around my body. I sit up, looking at my hands. They are a young woman's hands again. The shimmer of the light is pressing against my back, the voices getting louder, telling me it's all right. I am so close to the people that I love, I can sense them.

I close my eyes, stand up, and move from the light, back into the shadows. I will be with them soon enough. The light fades as I look down at my body, collapsed at the kitchen table, and I reach out to touch my head. Cold already. I realize that time truly does move differently for spirits. I lean down to my body and whisper, "Don't worry, I will join them soon. But first, I have to say goodbye to the kids."

I pause for a moment, a vision of Lillian suddenly entering my mind. This makes me hesitate, and I wonder what became of her soul when she died. Does she slip through dreams, as Lizzy once wondered? *Has she slipped through mine?* Surely, she must be at peace by now.

There is a knock on the door, and I move closer to see my home aide rummaging through her purse to find the key. It's a shame that she must find me dead, but I have to move on, and as she opens the door to come inside, I slip right by her and step outside. The wind lifts me up, and I shout with joy as I move on from one home, toward the next.

The End

About the Author

Amy Sampson-Cutler is a writer who earned her master's degree in Creative Writing from Goddard College. Her work can be found in *Tales to Terrify*, wow-women on writing, the Pitkin Review, Wellness Universe and Elephant Journal. Her writing focus is suspense, horror, poetry, science fiction, and the occasional love story.

She is the Executive Manager at Mount Peter Ski Area, where she grew up skiing in the winter and dreaming up stories in the summer. Her favorite days are spent knocking around story ideas with her husband. She lives in the Hudson Valley with her husband, son, and a ridiculous amount of furry family members. She can be contacted through AmysHippieHut.com.

Note from the Author

Word-of-mouth is crucial for any author to succeed. If you enjoyed *A Shadow of Love*, please leave a review online—anywhere you are able. Even if it's just a sentence or two. It would make all the difference and would be very much appreciated.

Thanks!
Amy S. Cutler

We hope you enjoyed reading this title from:

BLACK ROSE
writing™

CPSIA information can be obtained
at www.ICGtesting.com
Printed in the USA
BVHW072253190422
634739BV00014B/274